The Lost Village

DAVID GLOVER

The Lost Village

St. Martin's Press
New York

Library of Congress Cataloging in Publication Data

Glover, David, 1934-
  The lost village.

  I. Title.
PR6057.L626L6   1984   823′.914   84-13252
ISBN 0-312-49902-7

First published in Great Britain by Robin Clark Ltd.

First U.S. Edition

10 9 8 7 6 5 4 3 2 1

For Heather

The Lost Village

1

'He will want us to show him India,' said the sturdy young man lying on the bed. He stared at the dim, naked lightbulb. The room was narrow and high. Out of sight a pigeon walked onto one of the rafters, turned like a gymnast and paraded back to its nest through a hole in the wall. 'What treats will you show him, Arun?'

The slightly-built man addressed was preparing coffee. He jabbed two punctures in a tin of condensed milk, and darted his tongue over his lips before replying: 'We have had English masters before. They stay one year, two at the most. Let him find his own India.'

'Miss Willcox will perhaps be willing to show him,' said the first speaker.

'Miss Willcox is a part of India I reserve most definitely to myself,' said the coffee-maker, and plugged in the electric kettle.

The third occupant of the room, a middle-aged darker gentleman, moved uneasily in his chair, and pretended to examine the bookcase.

The first speaker raised himself to a sitting position in anticipation of the coffee, and continued: 'You and I, Arun, are general-purpose Indian English masters. Our guest here, Mr Mattacharya, is very much the Indian Indian mathematics master. Now the gentleman arriving here tomorrow is an English English master. Also, he will be head of English department, and therefore our master. Thus, what does that make him algebraically, Mattacharya Sahib, $2x^2$?'

'Ha, ha!' said the mathematics teacher. 'This sudden interest in algebra is most encouraging, Mr Panwar. But I will explain.' He raised his voice and spoke firmly as though addressing a class.

1

'If you are x, he cannot be x, let him be y.' There was a pause, but Mr Mattacharya had evidently finished.

Panwar picked up a stage sword from beside his bed, and twirled the weapon vaguely. 'So we are all unknown quantities. Arun there, a very ritualistic but time-consuming coffee-maker, is perhaps z like the waves of his alluring, shiny hair.'

'I demand to be z!' cried the coffee-maker. He began to dispense the condensed milk neatly into each cup. 'What's more I demand to be z to the power of ten.' Grinning at his room-mate, he added softly: 'Miss Willcox will confirm. Good!' He jerked up the tin above the last cup to prevent the sticky stream from making a mess. He stared with contempt at the specks of chicory floating on the surface, then handed the cup to his guest. 'At least this fellow will bring us some good quality English coffee. Nothing more is to be expected of him, save extra work. He will wish to make his mark on our happy, slack English department. Panwar there, who is so lazy that he even wants his coffee brought to him on his bed, is so worried, Mattacharya Sahib, about the impression his laziness will make on this new chap – a fellow with bright ideas to improve editorial content of the School Review. Its English language section will expand.'

The mathematics teacher's chair squeaked with agitation when he heard the subject of his visit mentioned so soon. 'Ah, the review,' he sighed, as if it were a bright but wayward pupil. 'Every fortnight Hindi section is getting shorter and shorter. We have a most able English department already, I think. This new man, an Oxford man and young, I hear, will cut hard at it.'

'Out, damn spot!' cried Panwar, and ferociously slashed the air. He got up and took his coffee with care and pleasure from the table, around which Arun still hovered frowning.

'No, Mattacharya Sahib,' said Panwar seriously as he regained his bed, 'we will resist him. Did we win independence from the British twenty-five years ago for nothing? No, the problem is lack of contributions for the Hindi section. We beg you, Mattacharya Sahib, to strain for contributions.'

'Could we enliven it with Sanskrit contributions?' asked Arun, looking innocent.

'Good,' laughed Panwar. 'House football matches reported in lively Sanskrit.'

2

The older man smiled at the frivolity of the young, and sipped his coffee gingerly.

While the three men were drinking their coffee, dumpy dark Miss Willcox, Christian and of low caste extraction, sat in the school nurse's little room attached to the clinic, situated about fifty yards from the quarters of the English department.

'This time,' said Miss Willcox brightly, 'I will have the Englishman. That is only fair.' The nurse raised her eyebrows; the effect was to increase the sick look of her long, sallow face. She turned away from Miss Willcox, and began to comb her hair which she had just washed.

'Mr Macgregor was Scotch,' the nurse answered. 'And not a catch at all. Old, always ill – the principal insisted I tend him often. It was a duty.'

Miss Willcox, emboldened by a second tot of medicinal Sikkim brandy, replied: 'Such a duty, till twelve midnight. How exhausted the poor man always looked after your nightly, nursey duty calls.'

'The position of nurse is always misunderstood in this country. But Mr Macgregor was brought up with Florence Nightingale thoughts. He had respect for my profession and for my person.' She tugged hard at a troublesome knot.

'You should wear it short; so much more fashionable now in England, and convenient in this dreadful climate.' The nurse continued tugging. 'I will bet you,' continued Miss Willcox impatiently and over-loud, 'that I will get this new man first. Come on now, how much – fifty rupees, one hundred rupees?'

'Non-ethical,' said the nurse. She shook out her hair, and began to brush it. 'Besides, in three days time he will have most terrible diarrhoea and vomiting from change of food and water. I shall be forced to go to him. What a pity you are so far away at the other end of the fort in the Junior School. He will have no duties in the Junior School. By force of circumstance I am on his doorstep.'

'Over it, you mean.'

'Such nonsense.'

'You forget, he will want to help with the many plays I produce. One hundred and fifty rupees?'

'If you are so set on him, have him for free. There, I give him to

3

you, free.' The nurse sat down, tossed her hair over the back of the chair, and closed her eyes. 'Your fiery beau, Arun Sen, how will he feel about all this?'

'What do I care how Arun Sen feels. Let him feel. I tell you confidentially, I am quite afraid for my reputation. Why, only the other day I was saying to dear Mrs Bhoshi, she who was with the poet-saint Tiganji in Nagpur, people will be thinking something.'

'Tell me, how does he make love?'

'I must really be going now. We have all talked enough silliness. How boring this ghastly place is, that we fuss over one wretched little Englishman.' She made getting-up movements.

'One for the road "afore ye go".'

'No, no, no. I should never find my way back.' She giggled and held a hand over her glass. The nurse got up and went to a cupboard.

'The nights are becoming chilly now. It is November 1st. You must take care to keep warm at nights. A little light brandy can be most beneficial.'

'One tiny, tiny glass then. No, no. Stop, stop. I shall start babbling.'

The nurse settled back and waited for the babbling to begin. But before this could happen, the two women were disturbed by the shouts of servants. The nurse got up and looked out of the window.

'There is great activity in front of the principal's bungalow,' she said. 'The vice-principal is coming out. The principal comes to the door and calls him back. The servants are hovering with the lamps. Now the principal is giving him some paper. He is hurrying off in this direction. Heavens! I think he is coming here. Give me the brandy quick. Here, take some tea leaves in your mouth. No, he is going on to Arun and Panwar's quarters. What has happened? You must find out from Arun.'

'How am I to find out? Am I just to go to his quarters in dead of night?'

Panwar had got off his bed, and was pacing the little room. 'But in spite of the inconvenience, you must admit, Mr Mattacharya, that he will get a beautiful first impression. The weather is cool now. The night air is scented with flowers. He will

4

have one full day to settle in, and then it will be Founder's Day. He will see the fort in all its glory. The visiting Maharajah. Our own Rajah and Rani. My play, *Macbeth,* in what a setting – battlements, moon. He will be enchanted.'

'He will laugh at Lady Macbeth's flip-flops,' said Arun. 'You have forgotten all about the shoes. The costumes are magnificent, but. . .'

'Well, the witches do not need shoes. Must I see to everything? Why did you not tell me before?'

'I was not asked.'

'You must plan most carefully,' said the mathematics teacher. 'And now I really must leave, I think.'

The jogging light preceding the vice-principal stopped outside Panwar and Arun's quarters, and whined: 'Panwar Sahib, vice-principal.' Mattacharya stepped back from the door, and the two young men attempted to tidy up.

The vice-principal entered. He was a small, round fat-faced man from the south of India. He resembled his principal in all these features. But unlike the principal, he was almost black. His name was Warri Banglaratnam, which gave rise to such nick-names as 'Worryguts' and 'The Bungler'.

'Ah!' he cried. 'Panwar, Sen, Mr Mattacharya I see. An editorial review conference. Excellent. You are preparing material and ideas for your new editor. Alas something terrible has happened to him. He is not coming on the seven up train tomorrow, but on the five up on the third morning. Here is a telegram from him. I will read it: "Fog London Airport. Now arriving 07.30 hours, 3rd." Read for yourselves.' He handed the telegram round.

'What is this fig at London Airport?' queried Mattacharya.

'Fig?' cried the vice-principal, grabbing back the telegram and scrutinizing it severely. 'No, no. That is just a transcription error. It means fog, clearly fog.'

'Fog or fig,' grumbled Mattacharya, 'is the delay so terrible? Does it really matter?'

The vice-principal waved the telegram impatiently. 'You do not understand. Mr Panwar, please explain.'

Panwar smiled and looked blank. 'It is inconvenient?' he hazarded.

5

'More than inconvenient,' broke in Arun Sen. 'This is the same train as that on which the Maharajah, our Founder's Day chief guest, arrives. It will be impossible to attend fully on the platform to both important guests at the same time. Moreover, the Englishman will see the journalists, flashbulbs and red carpet all popping off. He may think they are for him.'

'Exactly,' said the vice-principal. 'Of course I know English teachers. He will not be immodest. You forget, I taught chemistry for a whole year at Throgton School in Cheshire. We had the most appalling fogs at Throgton. Even when the apple trees bloomed there were fogs.'

'Were there fig trees at Throgton, too?' asked Panwar.

'No, no. It was too far north. In the south there are fig trees. But that is not really the point. The point is that the principal is most distressed. Our Englishman will be thrown straight into Founder's Day celebrations with hardly time to wash his face. The English department, all of us, must cushion the blow. We must have a plan. All of us must have a plan. No, Mattacharya Sahib, please don't go. We need your incisive mathematical mind. All arrangements must go like clockwork. He must not be allowed to feel less important than the Maharajah.'

'Why is he not being met at the airport?' asked Panwar.

'That is exactly the problem,' said Banglaratnam. 'His earlier telegram said, "Insist do not meet at airport. Will make own travel arrangements to school." These English I tell you are amazing. They are so independent. He will be in a strange country where all sorts of misfortunes may befall him, but he ventures forth alone. He may meet with an unsavoury type.'

'He may meet with a sweet type,' said Arun Sen.

'No, no. He is much more likely to meet an unsavoury type. He will get a bad impression. We must do something.'

While they deliberated, the outcaste servant allotted to the Englishman squatted beside the path outside. He chose a position at a respectful distance from the man who had lit the vice-principal's way. The outcaste would not speak to the other man; he waited hoping to learn something.

After five minutes, the lantern bearer addressed the night air. 'Your Englishman is not coming. He is dead.' The lantern was raised so that its light fell briefly on the outcaste's face. He

6

blinked and nodded his head down and to one side. The lamp was lowered, and its bearer continued: 'He was poisoned with unripe fruit by Chinese spies. All the passengers were poisoned. As the plane took off, it was immediately surrounded by a dense, black cloud of poison mist. The rest of the sky was clear, but the poison cloud stayed wrapping this one plane in evil. Then the poison of the fruit took effect. The pilot fought for control, but he was vomiting so much that he could do nothing. Down, down. All lost in the mountains of the north.'

The light fell once more on the outcaste's face, and he nodded that he had heard and was grateful for the consideration shown him.

The vice-principal and Mattacharya came out and went off with the bearer. The outcaste, Ram Swarup, stayed where he was. The moon, nearly full, began to rise. He wrapped an old army blanket closer round him. Now there would be no warm cast-off clothes. Even with the extra eight rupees a month from the Englishman, it would have been difficult to afford the dowry. He was unwilling to return to his hut and the harsh questioning of his wife. For a long time he stayed there while the moon rose high illuminating the battlements and the ruined temple. The langur monkeys who lived there became restless, and squabbled briefly. A cloud blotted out the moon, and he saw the outline of a woman crouching low and half running up the path. She stopped, hesitated, then quickly retraced her steps. The cloud passed, and in the woods below the battlements a peacock called and was answered by another, then a third. For another hour Ram Swarup stayed there until all was quiet. When the old cobra who lived close to his hut slowly crossed the path, Ram Swarup greeted him and wished him good hunting. The snake paused, hissed softly as though in answer, and continued on his way. Stiff and cold, Ram Swarup stood up and made his way home.

2

The only guidebook which bothers to mention Karatpore in any detail relates what it considers 'an interesting and colourful legend' concerning the foundation of its fort.

'According to popular legend, Sena Suj, petty chief and great hunter, one day climbed the hill on which the fort and school are now situated. Feeling extremely thirsty, he asked for a drink of water from an ascetic he found meditating nearby. The man was so angry at being disturbed that he went to a pool and brought him some water after cursing it. The liquid caused Sena Suj to be stricken on the spot with a terrible, shaking chill. The prince's dismay was boundless. He asked the man what he must do to break the spell. The ascetic replied that he must enlarge the pool and build a fort. This the prince did, but when he had finished, the ascetic could not be found, and Sena Suj remained shaking and shivering to the end of his days.

'Another legend relates that when Tamburlaine invaded India at the end of the fourteenth century, he came to a rocky eminence overlooking Karatpore Fort. He looked south, and wheeling his horse cried out to his vast host: "We venture no further into such an inhospitable land." Next day the host departed for central Asia. The eminence is called Tamburlaine's Horse, though few have seen its resemblance to a horse.

'There is only one entrance to the fort,' continues the guidebook, 'via the Bandar Paur (Monkey Gate) so called because a lifesize carving of the monkey god, Hanuman,

8

once decorated its arch. Gate and carving have long since disappeared, though a long piece of stone, said to be the tail of the god, can be seen in the museum near the railway station. Admission two rupees. Closed on Mondays.

'Moghul conquerors gave the fort a wide berth, and nothing historically significant happened to it until the First War of Independence against the British. During this war, the Rajah of Karatpore was bullied by neighbouring powerful maharajahs into mustering his small army to harass the British on their way north. One cannon was installed on the battlements and pointing out to the plain one hundred feet below. The Rajah's army held the fort stubbornly for a week, but the British did not come that way. When news arrived that the British had defeated the freedom fighters at a great battle to the north, most of the little army drifted away. On the ninth day, however, a squadron of East India Company Horse, led by one Captain Percy Bell of Paisley, rode unmolested through the Monkey Gate. News of this arrival caused panic among the remaining soldiers. They were endeavouring to turn the cannon round to face the invaders, when Bell and his troopers rode up. Bell ordered his squadron to dismount, set down their lances and sabres, and help the freedom fighters to swivel the piece. That task successfully completed, the combatants sat down together in the shade for a smoke and a chat. Soon the Rajah and his retinue arrived. The Rajah invited Bell to go pig-sticking with him. They became firm friends. To this day, the gun points in to the fort, and male members of the royal family of Karatpore have, in addition to their Indian names, those of Albert and Percy.'

Edward Burney Priestman, soon to be head of the English department at Karatpore Public School (most recent count: 201 boys), shut his guidebook. He stepped from the tonga hired at Karatpore station, and continued on foot towards the Monkey Gate. Though the gradient was not steep, he considered that the wretched horse had enough to do pulling his cases and the tonga-wallah. Its hooves slipped and clattered on the uneven

9

path. He walked beside the animal and the smell of its sweat and of the old creaking leather pleased him.

'So,' thought Edward Burney Priestman, 'not such a dashing entrance as that of Captain Bell, but no less surprising. What cannon I wonder shall I find to turn round? But find one I shall.'

The little procession, followed now by several small, grubby boys, passed through the non-existent Monkey Gate. Once on level ground, Priestman remounted the tonga, which continued at a steady clip-clop towards the south end of the fort and the school buildings constructed, according to the guidebook, from the partially dismantled battlements.

Down at the station, the express train supposed to be carrying Edward Priestman, and definitely carrying the Maharajah, was approaching the worried little group of vice-principal and English department. Further up the platform and presiding over a red carpet, stood the principal, the local Rajah and his retinue.

The local Rajah, Ananda Ravi Albert Percy Swarup Suj, knew and disliked the imminent Maharajah. He wondered how, even at this late stage, he could wriggle out of the agony of having to meet the man. 'The fellow will be so super-royal he will be intolerable,' thought the Rajah. 'He will say how splendid everything is, as though we had done well on parade. As for his idiot of a wife, she is so tall, silent and beautiful with her bored smile and drooping lids, that I am sure to say something foolish to her. A new English master is coming on the same train. I suppose I can duck out of meeting him. After all, I am a rajah. If only I were up flying myself in my little Piper Moth where none of them could touch me. As for this fool of a principal, who sweats revoltingly and keeps on treading on the carpet; if his new Englishman is only half as disastrous as the last, then I shall dismiss you, my little fat principal, and you know it. What you don't know is that if the Englishman is any good, is a sport and likes flying, then I shall make him principal over all your heads.'

The Rajah motioned to his ADC, a calm and pleasantly smiling young man, to have the carpet swept again. This was done, but straightaway several of the many reporters and cameramen, pushed from behind by others wanting to be near, spilled over on to the carpet. The Rajah closed his eyes and a flashbulb went off accidentally. A train whistle sounded in the distance.

The Rajah noticed that the large grey patch half way up the carpet and to one side was still visible. It had been made by the last elephant to grace his court. The incident had occurred during this very Maharajah's last arrival five years before. Percy Rajah had nearly fainted with embarrassment. Now, somebody would have to stand over it to conceal it. The Rajah eyed the sweating principal, and smiled to himself.

At the other end of the platform, the vice-principal was in a turmoil wondering whether he could find an excuse for joining the royal party or whether he should stay where he was. He wanted to be part of both greetings. 'We must have a plan,' he said to the air, and a man selling hot, sweet tea cried, '*Garam chai,* sahib,' and offered him a little flower-pot cup. 'No, no, no!' cried the vice-principal, and brushed the man off.

'How shall we recognize him?' asked Panwar.

'Perhaps,' said the mischievous Arun Sen to Panwar softly, 'he will be wearing his Oxford cap and gown.' But the vice-principal overheard.

'No, no. He will not be wearing cap and gown. You forget, I know Englishmen. He will be easily formal. He will wear a tie, but not cap and gown.'

'Ah, we will recognize him by his tie.'

'Yes, yes,' cried Banglaratnam testily. His mind, always open to suggestion, had become confused by the image of cap and gown.

Panwar worried about *Macbeth*. He fretted at the waste of precious rehearsal time. 'The shoes; nobody has shoes. The tape recorder jams. If the audience crowd the aisles, how will Burnham Wood get down to Dunsinane? Will anybody care? They will only want to be done with the thing. Already I have massacred the text for them. But the new man will care. He will laugh, and I shall be miserable for the rest of my life. I shall throw myself on his mercy.'

By the red rug, now covered with a film of white dust, the Rajah thought: 'I shall greet him with fire in my eyes. Did he win a Distinguished Flying Cross? He did not. If he says to me once

11

more anything like the last time, "Oh, you find flying amusing, do you? Yes, I suppose you would," I shall challenge him. "Oh," I shall say, "you find running around the country being a government minister amusing, do you? A minister in the government that would take away all your inheritance and has ruined me. Yes, I suppose you would." But I am a host. I will never say such a thing, no matter how rude he is. I shall remain impeccably polite. Perhaps I could take his wife and him up for a little spin. A victory roll or two would shake the stuffing out of them.' The Rajah giggled at this idea, and twirled the ends of his waxed moustache higher. The principal laughed in concert. Now most of the retinue began to laugh and chat. A photograph was taken, and the Rajah began to feel quite jovial. The train whistle sounded again much nearer.

The vice-principal, who had come up and was hovering and beaming behind the principal, coughed much louder than he had intended in order to attract the principal's attention. The Rajah and the principal frowned.

'What is it, Banglaratnam?' snapped the principal, without turning round.

'If I station myself here,' said Banglaratnam, his thick eyebrows bobbling up and down, 'I would probably catch sight of Mr Priestman early, and then be able to spot him and rush down the train and greet him. Or perhaps he and His Highness have already met on the train, and will come out together. That would be the best plan.'

'What are you on about, Banglaratnam? Anyway, the royal carriages are sealed.'

'Sealed, sealed, definitely sealed,' came a chorus of voices from the Rajah's retinue.

'Of course the royal carriages are definitely sealed,' agreed Banglaratnam. 'But perhaps His Royal Highness, hearing that there is an Englishman alone on the train, has taken him into his carriage to prevent him meeting with unsavoury types.'

'You could always station yourself on the elephant patch,' suggested the principal.

'No,' said the Rajah, who had been pretending not to listen. 'The elephant patch is for our principal. He will cover it very adequately.' The retinue laughed as did the principal, but he became very red in the face.

'Go back!' snarled the principal as Banglaratnam started to accompany him to the stain. 'And get off the carpet!'

Just then a school clerk came up to the principal and told him than an Englishman had been sighted on the fort.

'Banglaratnam, there is an Englishman on the fort,' said the principal.

'Who is this Englishman? What is this Englishman? Why is he there?'

'How am I expected to know? See, the train is coming.' The principal straightened his tie and moistened his lips. 'You must arrange it quickly. Arrange it.'

Banglaratnam hurried off down the platform, questioning the clerk. The clerk, however, had not himself seen the Englishman, and knew little about the matter.

'It is all a mistake,' said Banglaratnam to the clerk. 'He must be a stray tourist.' He rejoined the English department. 'An Englishman has been sighted on the fort,' he told them, as the train came into view. 'Could he have come by the seven up?'

'If,' said Panwar, 'he had caught the four up to Badashand, he could have changed at Hoddapore Junction, and caught the six down back.'

'Why on earth should he want to do that?'

'I'm sorry, I don't know why he should have done that.'

'It was very silly of him,' said Arun Sen.

'Quick,' said Banglaratnam, 'go and ask somebody if an Englishman arrived on the six down.' Panwar hurried off to the ticket office. 'With luggage,' shouted the vice-principal after him.

'Banquo's ghost perhaps?' suggested Arun Sen. 'But he was Scottish.'

'No, no. Mr Priestman is definitely English. We do not want any more. . .'

His words were drowned by the noise of escaping steam as the train eased into the station, and by the shouts of vendors and of the hopeful crowds of third-class passengers, who knew nothing of Maharajah or teacher, and only hoped to get aboard such a crowded train.

Panwar found it difficult to get through the crush, and became

13

separated from the others. Banglaratnam rushed up the side of the train telling Arun to go in the opposite direction.

'Is there an Englishman aboard?' shouted Banglaratnam through many windows, and was told that there was one further up, and that he had just got off. Struggling through the crowd, he came face to face with a tall, bespectacled and slightly stooping European in tee-shirt and sandals. Banglaratnam grabbed his hand and shook it vigorously, saying: 'I am Banglaratnam, the vice-principal. I am so very pleased to meet you.'

'Well, I certainly didn't expect to be met,' said the European in an accent which puzzled Banglaratnam. 'But I am constantly delighted by the hospitality shown one in this great country of yours by total strangers.'

'Marvellous! You didn't expect to be met. We always meet our masters.'

'I really appreciate that. But I don't want you to think of me as a master, just a friendly enquiring guest.'

'How beautifully you put it. But come out of the crush. Where is your luggage?'

'Oh, I've got someone taking care of that.'

'Marvellous!'

'I'm really hungry, though. If you'll excuse me I must get something to eat.'

'Oh, all that will be taken care of immediately. Come to the car.' Banglaratnam called to Panwar and Arun that they were to see to the new arrival's luggage.

'I know your trains wait a long time at stations,' said the European. 'Sometimes up to half an hour. But I feel I should get some food fairly soon.'

'It will take only a moment, and you are there,' said Banglaratnam, showing the car as though it were a magic carpet. 'The others will find their own way back.'

'I am most impressed by the way you people arrange things at Benquist, Colhoon and Patel,' said the stranger getting into the car. Banglaratnam heard only the words 'impressed' and 'Patel'.

'You have already heard of our Mr Patel? He is so efficient in the geography department.' The car began to weave through the crowded bazaar, adding its honks to the continuous roar of voices and the blaring of radios.

'I should say Mr Patel does a very fine job in that department; ferrying us here and there.'

'Do you know Throgton School in Cheshire? You must have heard of it. I taught there for a whole year.'

'In England? I know the Cheshire Cheese pub in London.'

'Yes, wonderful cheese in Cheshire! Still you will come to love our own cheeses! In the south of India there are wonderful cheeses. You must go to the south.'

'Could your people fit that into my schedule? It's fairly tight, you know.'

'Yes, yes. You will have plenty of time to go to the south. Everything will be arranged. You will stay with me.'

'I suppose we do have enough time for that food?'

By the time the mistake was discovered, and Banglaratnam had returned his guest to the station, the train had left. The very irate Texan refused to stay the night at the school. He was put up at great expense in the town's only western-style hotel, a two-storey affair whose room numbers began for some reason at '201', and where luggage-less and wifeless, he was bitten by bugs. In years to come, he would relate with pleasure how as a young man he had been abducted by Indians. Banglaratnam's list of nicknames received the additions of 'Ten Gallon' and 'The Rustler'.

But at the red carpet, the principal had been swept away from the elephant stain by the press of people. The Maharajah, held up by the crowd, stared at the stain, and said to the Rajah, 'It would be rather nice, don't you think, if there were another exit from your charming little station.'

'I really am desperately sorry,' said the Rajah, near to tears. And to the principal, he whispered sadly: 'Your post. You deserted your post.'

The principal shut his eyes and pretended that he was beside his favourite lake in the hills.

3

'So, this is to be my room,' thought Priestman. 'Too big really, thirty feet by twenty feet and what a height of ceiling – must be twenty-five feet at least.' *Chuck, chuck, chuck* went a gecko on the wall. 'A small bedroom off with a single rather dusty white mosquito net hanging over the bed from a kind of wooden cross.' He shook the net, and had to blow out of his nostrils sand-tasting dust. Two trapped mosquitoes buzzed inside the net. 'Small dark boxroom for my trunks. Airy good bathroom. And from the main room, a verandah at the back leading on to a small garden.' He stepped on to the verandah and was startled by the flapping and cawing of several crows which he had disturbed pecking at something small and unrecognizable. The crows made off to join others in the trees and on the roofs. 'Constant cawing like living in the middle of a rookery. At the far end of the garden is a tap on a standpipe where chattering women and girls are filling pots and large, square tins. One girl really beautiful. They stop talking to watch me, then continue louder and laughing. A tree beside the pipe. A flock of green parrots performing acrobatics, dashing off shrieking, then dashing back again, like a lot of crazy school children screaming in a playground. And all playing tag with three striped squirrels who scuttle up and down the tree trunk. Beyond all this the servants' quarters. The smell of spices being cooked, making my face prickle. Beyond all that, a flat-topped hill like the one I am on. Tamburlaine's Horse, I suppose. I wonder whether I should shower before the welcoming committee arrives? "No, put the big case in the little room." So this is to be my servant I suppose. Bit scruffy. Bustling, beaming and bowing constantly among the cases. Must teach him not to be so obsequious. "Yes, that's right. Put it over there."

'How does all this fit me? How do I fit it? Will we learn to fit each other? What events and people will modify these first impressions? They are the best, gathered before one has bearings. Impressions that will remain despite later feelings about the place. The first magic of strange places. And do I recall anything, having left India at the age of three? No. A blanket is drawn over all that. All this is now.

'Yes, the place has possibilities. That little garden with its patches of coarse grass and weeds and the remains of some hedge like privet, I will cultivate. I will find out about the local plants. There must be some nursery in the town below. I will browse there, and everything will be so cheap. "One of this and one of that," I shall say. And in a few weeks, thick fleshy leaves and red and blue trumpet-shaped flowers will flap and dangle in the gentle breeze.

'Best of all is the verandah. It faces west so that I shall be able to watch the sun setting over that hill – pity it is so flat with no building or even a tree on it. I shall sit here in a cane chair with my sundowner, thankful for the cool breeze – showered and relaxed. The scent of flowers will be thick in the night air. One or two friends will drop in, and I shall mix them drinks. What I need is a sort of bar out here. Something quite long, with wicker front and sides, and four posts supporting a thatched roof. Some might think it pretentious, but one could almost imagine the sea quite close. All this faded green woodwork I could paint a rich medium blue. Yes, I can turn the whole verandah into a sort of South Seas relaxation area.

'This reception party is taking a long time to arrive. Perhaps I should have that shower. No. Here comes refreshment.'

Tea and little sweet cakes were brought by a splendidly handsome servant in a turban. He stood protectively by while Edward drank and devoured all the little cakes. Edward considered the scene. 'Just like the label on those bottles of liquid coffee essence called Colonel's Bivouac or something. All the scene needs is sabre and topee casually flung on a nearby chair, then I shall feel like my grandfather Priestman, hero of the Punjab.

'Of course, the setting demands the arrival of an appropriate female who will be appropriately impressed by the sight of me in it. I suppose most young bachelors look at any new place they are in with an eye to its possibilities for seduction. I expect spiders and fish do the same, so we are in good company; I can relax having satisfied the scientific as well as the romantic in me. The moralist in me will have to wait for a few years, then I shall satisfy him. Meanwhile I shall do a thoroughly good job. Change a few things though not hurriedly. Get the department moving smoothly.'

Priestman had just finished his shower when the reception committee arrived. He met them in his dressing-gown. There seemed to be about twelve of them bobbing and shifting before him. They were roughly formed up in two ranks. Individuals from the rear rank broke through the first as they were introduced by the principal, then they slipped back again, like some old-fashioned musketry manoeuvre.

'This is Mr Singh. This is Mr Thing. This is Mr Blankashah.' Present hand, shake, discharge smile, retire.

'I am so sorry you were not met,' said the principal. 'But you said you were coming on the five up.'

'Oh, I thought I didn't actually specify a particular train. I didn't know their times until I arrived in Delhi.'

'Oh, it doesn't matter. We are so glad that you have arrived at last.' There was a chorus of nods. 'This is Founder's Day, and tonight you will be entertained. *Macbeth,* I believe isn't it, Mr Sen, Mr Panwar? They muttered assent.

'Can I help backstage?'

'Oh no,' said the principal. 'Please just watch and enjoy. Is everything alright?' The principal looked dubiously around the room. 'Mr Banglaratnam, our vice-principal, is a trifle detained in town at the moment, but he will see to anything you require.'

4

The brightly-lit stage was a wooden platform temporarily erected just below an intact section of battlement. To its left, looked at from the audience, was a towering disused temple in semi-darkness. Its architectural form suggested a squat Mayan pyramid that had gone on a diet to attain the model elegance of a Burmese pagoda, but had given up half way through the course. Decorative, possibly copulatory, figures had been defaced or eroded.

The front row of the audience consisted of a central block, or cockpit, of Maharajah, Maharani, Rajah and principal. From either side spread royal relations and aides until the wing tips were reached where lesser mortals such as Banglaratnam perched briefly or hopped about awaiting summonses from within.

One chair at the centre was empty, having been vacated by the Rajah's wife during the introductory songs in praise of her dead father-in-law, the old Rajah and founder of the school. It was her invariable social duty on such occasions almost to break down at the mention of the old Rajah. She would stand up suddenly, her head shaking in distress, and stumble away with sweeping strides awkward for such a small woman. An anguished almost weeping retinue would accompany her to the car.

Now back in the palace, the Rani relaxed with a little bottle of elixir, popped a sweetmeat into her mouth, switched on the radio for her favourite music programme, and settled down to munch her way through a ninth re-reading of *War and Peace;* 'It's the only book,' she was fond of repeating. The old Rani, a little bird-like woman of ninety, and bent nearly double, popped her head round the door.

19

'How did it go, dear?' she squeaked. She had formerly performed the ritual.

'This year I almost fainted at the car door, mother-in-law.'

'The Rajah would have been proud. You are a credit to this house and to me,' said the old woman, and popped out again.

After the Rani's departure, the festivities could properly begin. It was Banglaratnam's hope that one day he would be invited to occupy the Rani's vacated chair. During the interval before *Macbeth* began, the principal called Banglaratnam to him. Banglaratnam put a hand on the back of the chair, and rested one foot on its supporting strut, which snapped back a sharp protest. He straightened up quickly.

'Banglaratnam, please don't break the chair,' said the principal. 'Kindly have it removed so that we may all spread out a little.'

'Aha!' said Banglaratnam as though he had just hit upon a brilliant plan. 'If perhaps I were stationed adjacent to you, sir, I would then know your requests sooner, and be able to take notes promptly. I see. Very well. I will have it removed immediately. Though if it were pulled back slightly, I would be almost behind you and to your right at, say, an angle of forty-five degrees looked at in plan. Ah.'

He called a servant who removed the chair to the end of the row where Banglaratnam seated himself upon it sadly, his thick eyebrows raised.

'For days,' said the Maharajah to his wife, 'I shall go around looking at the sky, because this stage is so high. Do you remember how at that real school we went to they had a proper amphitheatre from which one looked down at the stage?'

'Oh, yes. And do you remember how we saw *Antigone* there? Such an elegant Greek play. I was really moved.'

'Of course, it was produced by their resident English master. It helps so much with clarity of diction.'

The Rajah overheard. 'We have a resident English master too, you know. An Oxford man.'

'Really?' said the Maharajah with genuine surprise. 'When did he arrive?'

'Today. By the same train as yours.'

'What a pity you didn't tell me. It would have been so pleasant

20

to have had an educated man as travelling companion. My wife, you know, was saying during all that boring journey that what we really needed was an educated Englishman to entertain us. What college was he at I wonder? Magdalen? I was at Trinity.'

Percy Rajah turned to the principal.

'Why didn't the Englishman travel with the Maharajah?'

'There were certain uncertainties, sir.' The principal snapped his fingers, and Banglaratnam was there. 'Why did you not arrange for Mr Priestman to travel with the Maharajah?'

'There was the fog problem. And the question of the American who had to be looked after.'

'Oh, we all know you found an American. Don't dwell on it. Go and find Mr Priestman. Why is he not here with us?'

'You said he was to. . .'

'Never mind that. Go and bring him.'

Banglaratnam dashed off. He returned as the first clap of thunder cracked from the tape recorder.

'He has disappeared,' wailed Banglaratnam.

'You have lost him again!' cried the principal.

'When shall we three meet again?' screamed the First Witch.

Priestman had joined Panwar and Arun Sen backstage. Priestman said that he would act as trouble shooter, and Panwar was relieved that he was not actually watching the performance. Everything seemed to be going well.

Enter Lady Macbeth and messenger on battlements.

LADY MACBETH. What is your tidings?

MESSENGER. The king comes here tonight.

LADY MACBETH. You bring great news. *(Exit messenger)*

The raven himself is hoarse

That croaks the fatal entrance of Duncan

Under my battlements.

(SOUND: *Raven off*)

The sound of 'raven off', actually a tape recorded common house crow, alarmed a peacock under the battlements. It shrieked, and was answered by a second, then a third. The audience giggled.

'A flock of hoarse ravens!' remarked the Maharajah to Percy Rajah. 'Most inventive.'

'Thank you,' said the Rajah.

21

SCENE VI *Before the castle*

Enter Duncan, Malcolm, Donalbain, Banquo, Lennox, Macduff, Ross, Angus, etc.

(LIGHTING: *Bring up spot 2 on temple (castle) as Duncan and Banquo's speeches proceed*)

DUNCAN. This castle hath a pleasant seat: the air
Nimbly and sweetly recommends itself
Unto our gentle senses.

BANQUO. This guest of summer,
The temple-haunting martlet, does approve

(PROPS: *Draw cardboard bird on wire round temple*)

(LIGHTING: *Bring up spots 2 and 3 full on temple*)

However, instead of a house martin, three very large disturbed fruit bats emerged from the temple. Blinded by the light, they beat round the building dodging the cardboard bird.

Panwar was distraught. 'Arun, Arun! You told me all the bats were gone. Are you the stage manager or what?'

'Was I to climb up there with a stick? Anyway, some probably came back.'

'Ruined. Ruined. All is lost!'

Back in the front row, the Maharajah said to his wife: 'What an amusing idea to make *Macbeth* a black comedy. Castle Dracula, I assume.'

'Do remember all the details, darling,' said the Maharani. 'It will make a super story for our party on Tuesday. By the way, is the prime minister coming?'

'Refuses to miss it, I gather. I wonder if they will make the porter Duncan's murderer. But we are still in the animal circus stage. Tell me, Percy, do you bring on an elephant in act three, perhaps?'

'There are no more elephants at Karatpore, I think,' said the Rajah, and whispered to the principal: 'Swear to me on your life that there are no elephants.'

'No, I think there are definitely no elephants. At least there are none in the programme.'

'All these birds and bats, Percy,' said the Maharajah, 'so reflect your interest in flying. I must say I am glad you are sitting here with us. Otherwise, you might suddenly appear in your. . .kite, is it? Yes, and swoop down on us to finish the play.'

22

A *deus ex machina* or rather a *rajah ex machina*, ha, ha!'
'That reminds me,' said the Rajah. 'I was wondering whether you and your dear wife would care to come up with me for a little spin tomorrow?'

'Not for the world, dear boy. Neither of us can abide the thought of flying.'

'Just a ten minute little hop?'

'Alas, no. But look at your play.'

Enter Lady Macbeth.

DUNCAN. See! See! Our honour'd hostess

Out of the temple ran a frightened young monkey. It made to jump over the battlements, but its way was blocked by Lady Macbeth. It dodged back out of sight behind the temple. The audience burst into shouts and hoots.

'You assured me, Sen!' cried Panwar. 'You assured me. Now he will be popping out throughout the rest of the play. Ruined. Mr Priestman, I am so sorry.'

'Nonsense. It was a splendid idea to stage the play here. We shall do *Hamlet* here, and damn the audience.'

Enter Macbeth.

MACBETH. If it were done, when 'tis done, then 'twere well
It were done quickly.

'Good idea,' said Priestman. 'Give me a stick, keep the lights off the temple. I'll go up and get it out.'

He began to climb. But though the stage lights were dimmed, the moon had risen, and he could be seen quite clearly edging his way round and up. The boys cheered, and began to stamp and shout in unison. 'See! See! Our honoured hostess!'

'Look at our Englishman,' said the Rajah proudly. 'Doesn't fear heights. Go on, that's the way!'

'This is dreadful!' cried the principal. 'Banglaratnam. Where the devil are you? He must be stopped. We have paid his fare. He may have a prang.'

'Have a what?' snapped the Rajah.

'Prang?' suggested the principal meekly.

'That is an air force term with very precise meaning. Don't use words you don't understand. He's gone round the other side!' shouted the Rajah to Priestman. 'Anyway, what's this damn play about?'

23

'About Macbeth and his wife who murder their guest, Duncan, that's the king, and Macbeth becomes king.'

'Happy times. Shakespeare is it? How does it end?'

'Macbeth is killed by the rightful heir to the throne.'

'Probably the government made him end it like that.'

Priestman edged out of sight round the temple. The monkey came quickly round to the front.

'See! See! Our honoured hostess,' chanted the boys.

Lady Macbeth was pacing vigorously up and down the battlements, for which the monkey made a dash, brushing against her. She shoved it away with a cry. It dived over the battlements, and was gone. The audience let out a rousing cheer. Lady Macbeth, looking rather green, lent silent against the wall.

'Go on, go on, Ashok,' prompted Panwar. 'I would while it was smiling in my face.'

'Is there more?' wept the Maharajah. But in the event, the rest of the performance contained no spurious elements.

Dumpy, dark Miss Willcox said to her friend the nurse: 'Wasn't he marvellous? Wasn't he brave? Arun just hovered about on the ground while Mr Priestman performed such feats of daring. He is the sort of Englishman who climbs Mount Everest totally without oxygen.'

'It was rather stupid of him,' said the nurse. 'You forget. Had he fallen I would have had to tend his broken legs.'

'Did you hope for that?'

'Silly. I just mean that that adventurous young man is soon going to get himself into trouble. And cost me extra work.'

'Get you into trouble, if you're not careful.'

They got up and began to leave together with the rest of the audience. 'You know, something very strange was said to me about him,' said Miss Willcox. 'When he was climbing down, Mrs Bhoshi, she who was with the poet-saint Tiganji in Nagpur, whispered to me, "There is a large element of holiness in that man, but he will not recognize it, and that will cost him and us dear." '

The nurse laughed: 'Your silly old Mrs Bhoshi sees the saint in everybody, especially if they happen to be clasping a temple at the time.'

'Well, is that a bad thing? But you're wrong about her, she's

24

very perceptive about people. And she's always right.'

'And do you want to find the holiness in him?'

'Oh, you're such a cynic,' said Miss Willcox. 'You don't understand me at all. I take just one little drink, and then I feel in a betting mood. I know I was stupid the other night, but drink and betting are occupational hazards of Catholicism.'

Miss Willcox, who had been brought up largely by Irish nuns of a rather modern order, sighed at the burdens put upon her by religion. She reflected that she had not gone to communion two days ago on All Saints Day. She tried to convince herself that it was because she had had a drink after midnight. Suddenly she longed to be back in bed, to think about the Englishman with pure, gentle thoughts, to say the Our Father and the Hail Mary. Then to sleep; sound in the knowledge that she had prepared herself well for confession next morning. She would really intend amendment. She would not commit fornication again. She would never see Arun Sen again. Never again save in company. The words 'act of contrition' and 'absolution' repeated themselves in her brain.

'Look,' said the nurse, 'your splendid Englishman is coming this way. Perhaps Arun will introduce you.'

'No, no! You don't understand,' said Miss Willcox, and hurried away to catch up Mrs Bhoshi. And Priestman, summoned to the royal party, continued on his way, smiling quite royally himself and saying 'thank you' to the many people who showered congratulations upon him.

The members of the royal party stood beside their cars.

'Good at heights,' said the Rajah to Edward.

'Actually, sir, I must admit that I detest them.'

'How was your flight?' asked the Maharajah grinning. He swayed slightly as though drink in hand on Trinity lawn.

'Frightful!' responded Priestman, biting his lower lip then pushing the word out in the approved party-going manner. 'Touristic elements amusing enough. A succession of rich bored-looking merchants in a succession of Middle Eastern transit lounges. Have you noticed how it is always 2 a.m. in a transit lounge? But the trouble is, I dislike flying. I can't understand how the beastly things stay in the air.'

'One fault,' said the Maharajah laughing, 'and they don't. Did

25

you hear that Percy? How do they stay up?'

'It is a question of aerodynamics,' said Percy Rajah heavily.

'No doubt,' said the Maharajah. 'But should aerodynamics be allowed to assault the human psyche?'

'It is assaulted enough without aerodynamics,' said Priestman.

'You really must try and visit us in the holidays soon,' said the Maharajah.

'Yes, why don't you do that? We will write to you,' said the Maharajah's beautiful wife, lightly touching his sleeve as she got into the car.

Among the thorn bushes which surrounded the little hollow where the cast had dressed and applied their make-up, Priestman's servant, Ram Swarup, still squatted with his daughter and the other servants. They stared at the empty stage and the magnificent costumes of the cast who were reluctant to disperse, and so end an occasion that had dominated their thoughts and emotions for so many weeks. They milled around in the hollow, and irritably teased each other or prodded one another with stage weapons, all the time uttering snatches from the play.

'Did you see what a fine man your father serves?' said Ram Swarup to his daughter.

'It was cruel to frighten the monkey people and the bat people,' said the girl. 'The temple is their home. Our Nag Rajah would not have been frightened by a Englishman with a stick. He would have raised his head, spread his hood, and spat at him as he spat at old staggering Redhead.'

Her father smiled, remembering how Macgregor had come upon the snake, and how quickly he had sobered up and backed away, eyes bulging and mouth open.

'We must make offerings,' continued the girl, whose name was Amanti. 'And pray to Hanuman that he will forgive us for disturbing his people.'

Ram Swarup was filled with pride at the thought that this was his daughter, and that she alone, and not all those other great and careless people, had known and said what was right to do. They made their way slowly home. 'No,' he thought, 'I have not waited so long in vain to betroth you, my beautiful little correct daughter. Why, even when the holy man, Agrawal, who is

26

revered throughout the world, visits the fort, it is you, daughter, he loves to speak with most. I shall make a really worthy match for you. And I think I have found the man. Soon we shall know.'

5

After the play, Priestman sat with Panwar and Arun Sen in their room, and drank coffee.

'Cheer up, Panwar,' said Priestman. 'All the things you thought would go wrong, didn't. And nobody noticed the lack of shoes.'

'You are being too kind. But if it is always the unexpected that happens, how can one ever prepare?'

'You are too involved, Panwar,' said Arun. 'But really, Mr Priestman. . .'

'Edward, please. But not Ted if you don't mind.'

'Well, Edward,' continued Arun. 'Your help was invaluable.'

'Nonsense. You would have managed well enough without me.' Priestman looked round the dreary room containing little more than Panwar's bed, the chair that he himself was sitting on, and the coffee table. On its lower shelves were exercise books for marking, and one or two bound volumes. Another room, little bigger than a cupboard and smaller than the box room for Edward's trunks, gave off the main room. It was evidently Arun Sen's bedroom since various items of clothing were visible on a low couch constructed from a tin trunk covered with a mattress. Cooing and fluttering came occasionally from somewhere aloft. A single feather floated slowly down and landed on one of Panwar's flip-flops. Priestman vowed that he would enquire of the principal if these wretched quarters could not be improved.

'Perhaps the holes in the roof could be bunged up to keep out the pigeons?' suggested Priestman.

'But where would they go?' asked Panwar.

'This one is a wild Indian,' thought Priestman. 'The other one is relatively tame.'

'Now he is frowning,' thought Panwar. 'Already I wonder how

28

my score stands with him. I can remember every word we have exchanged since we met earlier today. The trembling, physical trembling, in my legs as I said this thing and that thing, how he reacted to my every statement. I think "how can I recoup that frown, that raising of the eyebrows?" I try desperately to remain calm, almost offhand, but it is the first time that I have met an Englishman, and I even find it difficult to understand his accent. All the time, Arun who thinks he knows them because he met Macgregor, chatters on, laughing, gesticulating, making a great impression, even leaning forward to tap him lightly on the knee. No that was a mistake. Edward recoils slightly and frowns. Arun sees. He moistens his lips, but goes on talking, joking about lions and tigers.'

'And near my home village in Bengal,' continued Arun Sen, 'there are many tigers. How marvellous to find that you too, Edward, are so interested in wild life. But there you may also meet the king lion.'

'But I thought the only lions left in India were a few protected in the Gir forest?' queried Priestman.

'No, no,' said Arun Sen. His tongue flipped quickly over his lips. 'No, these are not ordinary lions. I am talking about the king lion. He is very rare.'

'He must be. I've not read about him in the books on the subject. What does it look like? Striped or plain tawny? Has it a mane? What sort of country does it inhabit? Jungle or open plains?'

'Poor Arun,' thought Panwar. 'He has never considered any of these things. But he has got himself in too deep now.'

'Oh, jungle, jungle. And as to its colour, you must understand that I have not personally come face to face with it. At least, not by daylight!'

'And at night?'

'Then I tell you I was frightened out of my wits!'

He launched into a long rambling story of torches, terrified villagers and ferocious roaring. Priestman smiled from time to time, though he tried not to. Arun Sen, noticing this, began to clown and elaborate ridiculously. The story disintegrated into banter between them and bouts of laughter.

'And you, Panwar?' enquired Priestman when the story was

finished. 'Where do you come from? Are there king lions there?'

'I come from that part of India now called Pakistan. My parents, who are teachers too, took me from there as a baby when they were forced to flee the rioting at Partition. I'm afraid we had no lions or tigers there.'

'They have only mysterious practices there,' interjected Arun Sen. 'And a great love of the fair skins of either sex in their high, barren mountains. That is because they are descended from the lost Greek soldiers of Alexander the Great. Are you not, Panwar?'

'There are such tales,' said Panwar miserably. 'Now he is beginning to disgrace me,' thought Panwar. 'I know what Arun is hinting. And Edward thinks me a bore.'

'That's very interesting,' said Priestman looking serious. 'I was here at Independence too, though I don't remember anything. I was just three when we left. The first thing I remember in my life is the boat going home to England. I'm told we moved around the country a lot in the last two years. They say I used to babble away in half a dozen different Indian languages learnt from a succession of nannies. I'm told there was rioting and famine in several places where we stayed. So if it all comes back to me suddenly, I might start babbling at you in baby-talk Hindi!'

'So you have come home to the land of your birth,' cried Arun Sen. 'This is marvellous. You are one of us.'

'One had to return. Sometimes I would think I had dreamed about it. I wanted to find out if a visit would bring India all back to me. But no luck. My family have always had something to do with India. There was always talk of it at home. And of course I've read quite a lot. Hence my knowledge of wild life.'

'But seriously, Edward,' continued Arun Sen. 'Since you are so interested in wild life I can arrange a hunting expedition for you from my village. It will be the holidays soon. You must come and stay with me in Bengal. Please say that you'll come. All my family are dying to meet you, and you will be so comfortable.'

'That's marvellous. I really would like nothing better. The trouble is that Mr Banglaratnam – I hope I've pronounced that right. . .'

'Nobody can. It is not important. He is only here to give an "all-India" flavour to the school.'

'Ha! Well, he has already invited me to stay with him in the south.'

'You must go to the south,' chanted Arun imitating the vice-principal's accent, bulging out his eyes, and bobbing his eyebrows up and down. 'No, no, you cannot possibly do that. It is so hot there, and you will be so bored among all those savage Telegus and Madrasis. But you cannot go. There is not enough time these holidays. He must mean in the long vacation. But you will not be happy. They do not understand Englishmen and their needs. But in Bengal we have the longest and most understanding relationship with the English.'

'Yes, I've heard that. So, fine. . . Oh blast! I've just remembered, the Maharani invited me to go and stay with them these holidays, I think.'

'Oh, the great royal people. They will snap you up at a click of their little fingers, and you will be lost to us for ever.'

'What do you think, Panwar?' asked Edward. 'Do you think she will write and confirm it?'

'These maharajahs and such are very prone to their own whims. I hate them,' replied Panwar, voicing one of his very few strong opinions, then blushing at his words.

'But if she writes,' said Arun Sen, 'then you must not miss the opportunity. She is a real beauty, don't you think? And spoilt with Western education. And her husband is much older than her. I think, Edward, that she likes you very much.'

'What nonsense,' said Edward.

'But you were so brave, so English. And she touched your sleeve.'

'If she writes, then I suppose I must go. If not, then you'll have to put up with me.'

'Splendid,' said Arun, 'and in the meantime, we can explore all the jungle in this area. I tell you, Edward, I have been here over two years now, and I have not yet explored it. Panwar there, a more recent acquisition, is too lazy to get off his *charpoy* on Sundays, and till today there has been nobody here I would feel safe to go with. It is a very wild area full of dacoits, sorry I mean bandits, and other things. It is a very backward part being a native state before Independence, and with hardly any British influence.'

31

'It sounds exciting. Just the sort of place I was looking for. When shall we set out?'

'Why not this coming weekend?'

'Why not indeed.'

'This coming weekend,' said Panwar, 'is the Bhonsa sports day. The principal and everybody are going. I expect they will want you to go.'

'I, for one, shall certainly not go,' said Arun Sen.

'I see. But tell me, what is this Bhonsa sports day?'

'Oh, it is so boring. I went last year. Bhonsa is a village a few miles from here. It is supposed to be *our* village sponsored by the school, and with contributions by the boys to show that they all care desperately about the plight of poor rural India. There are embarrassing, long speeches in praise of our Percy Rajah, who most of the villagers think still rules them, and in praise of the government whose representatives none of them see except for election and tax purposes. Then there are some games. Then one wanders about the village looking at the fresh whitewash and the children scrubbed for the only time in the year. You must try to duck it.'

'What do you think, Panwar. Are you going?'

'Yes, I think I should go.'

'Then I will go. And instead of being bored, you can be my guide and tell me what everything means.'

'Yes, of course,' said Panwar wondering how he would manage because the local dialect was such a strange form of Hindi he could hardly understand the villagers, and knew next to nothing of their customs about which Edward was bound to ask.

'But the following weekend is ours,' insisted Arun Sen. 'When together we shall hack our way deep into unknown jungle. Which it really is you know.'

'It's a date, whatever happens,' said Priestman firmly. 'And now I really must go to bed. You see, I can't stop yawning. And I'll remember to write off for that coffee first thing in the morning.'

Priestman left, watched unbeknown to him by Ram Swarup who was fearful lest his new master take the path leading to the back of his quarters, and so risk an encounter with the snake. But Priestman went to the front entrance, and when Ram Swarup heard the inside wire-netted door bang, he went back to his own quarters and his wife.

They sat in their tiny low-ceilinged hut which was part of a long block inhabited by all the untouchables attached to the school. A curtain divided the room, and behind it their daughter Amanti tried to sleep. Recently, she had found it increasingly difficult to do so until her parents finished their nightly argument.

Ram Swarup felt the cold of November, but it was pleasant to draw the old blanket tighter round him, and to sip the warm, sweet tea. Now it was pleasant, too, to wait for his wife's habitual question, 'when will you betroth our daughter?' because this time he had an answer.

'So the new Englishman has come,' she began.

'He has come.'

'They say he is young, tall, and has curly golden hair and light blue eyes, that he jumps up and down temples like a monkey, and strides about laughing and joking. They say that the foolish teacher women of the Junior School have sweating palms at the thought of him.'

'They say! It is always "They say". I know nothing of these things, nor should you.'

'You see nothing beyond the end of your broom.'

'Because I attend to my work, I have been given to him.'

'And you must guard him well, or he will make a fool of himself with the women, and be sent away. Then where are your seven rupees a month from him?'

'Eight. And he gave me eight annas for fetching him cigarettes. He smokes a lot.' Ram Swarup smiled inwardly, and watched his wife with satisfaction as she drew the dress around her face and looked away.

'Peole who smoke do bad things.'

'That is only in Hindi films. Englishmen are different. The principal and vice-principal are overjoyed with him.'

'New brooms. And what will become of our daughter if he dies of smoke, drink and nurses like the old red-haired one? Next month our daughter will be fourteen years old, and still not betrothed. People look sadly at her. Other children make fun of her. I am ashamed for our clan, our family and ourselves. And most of all I am ashamed before the gods. Do you want the consummation ceremony before the betrothal?'

'You know nothing. Nowadays people are betrothed much later; and marry much later.'

'So say you, who listen to upper caste talk.'

'Do you not want to improve yourself, and have our daughter marry well?'

'Have her marry at all is all I say.'

'Now be quiet and listen. The barber says there is a man. . .'

'The barber is an old woman. He would not recognize a man if he saw one. Besides, when did barbers ever act as matchmakers for our clan? Other castes stopped using barbers for that years ago. Now they are glad of our business. They would not stoop to it before. And you are taken in.'

'Your teeth stick out farther than your tongue, which reaches to Tamburlaine's Horse. And your skin would frighten Ravana's army of devils back to Sri Lanka. My daughter has fine, even, white teeth and a fair skin like me. She will marry well.'

'Ah, first it is smoke he threatens me with, now it is teeth and skins. Perhaps you would have her marry a tanner, you are so interested in skins.'

'Are you not ashamed to disgrace your ancestors with such disrespect to your husband? Ah, if only my mother still ruled in this house.'

'Ahah! Now it comes out. I was wondering how long it would take you to bring your mother into it. And you call this a house? I, who left my father's mansion. . .'

'Enough, enough. Now listen to this. The richer the man we serve, the more prestige and honour we gain. Therefore the better the match we can make for our daughter. . .'

'Now he lectures me like a health visitor.'

'Quiet. For the first time I serve an Englishman. He is the very best sort of Englishman, too. I heard the principal say to the vice-principal as they came out of the Englishman's rooms, "that is the very best sort of Englishman".'

'And he is thirty if a day, and still not married. Perhaps you would have our daughter marry him. Is that your plan?'

'Oh great god Hanuman!' yelled Ram Swarup. 'I cry to you for succour in the hour of my trial. What hideous sins did I commit in former lives to be so stricken in this?'

And a neighbour cried out in anguish: 'Oh great god Hanuman, deliver us all from these shrieking devils of the night, and send us your blessed gift of sleep!'

Ram Swarup went outside; he squatted down and drew the blanket over his head. Then he spat long and noisily, and the neighbour let out a groan. Ram Swarup lit a *bidi* cheroot, which being little more than an inch long, he cupped in his fist, dragging the smoke out between his fingers.

'Nag Rajah,' he whispered, 'let me offer myself to you as a sacrifice, for surely that way I shall be delivered from my fate, and gain merit. Or if you will not have me, then talk to the great python who patrols the no-man's-land between Senior and Junior Schools. Say that if he does not wish to hunt again till after the festival of Holi, then I am his meal. Or perhaps I should climb down the battlements to where the leopards lie in wait for stray dogs. I shall go on all fours, whining and raising my leg among the thorn bushes. And that will be the end of me, for I am nothing better than a bald pye dog who bites his scabby back in the dust, kicked and cursed as I am by family and friends.'

In the hut, Ram Swarup's wife listened at the curtain.

'Are you awake, daughter?'

'Yes, mother, I am awake.'

Her mother drew the curtain aside, and looked at the serious but calm face of her daughter. Yes, it was true. She was beautiful. Her mouth is my mother's, thought Ram Swarup's wife, and something about the eyes is from my own grandfather, who could read.

'Do not look so sad, Amanti. Your father is a good man. But it is a wife's job to bully good men or they would do nothing. You will be betrothed soon. It will all be alright, so why look so sad?'

'It is not that which saddens me, but the thought that if my brother had lived, you and my father would not have had all this trouble. For then girls' fathers would have come to us seeking his hand for them. And there would have been many, because he was a fine young man.'

Her eyes filled with tears, and her mother put out her hand, and stroked her hair.

'You always think of others. You are an example and a treasure to us, and we are blessed in you.' The mother knelt by

35

the bed and shed tears. After a moment, she continued. 'But you should not cry, you who are so bold and strong as well as kind. Why, last year I caught you still clambering over the old cannon. And when you were eight, you ran naked with the boys through the first rain of the monsoon, and plunged with them into the tank. Oh what a stir it caused, and me shouting by the side of the tank for you to come out, and shaking your dress at you, and that old red-haired devil laughing and watching shamelessly.'

'I have the wish still to swim, to run, and to go places and see things. Only three times, mother, have I been out of this place in all my life, and then only to the town. I envy the school boys when they go away for holidays.'

'Yes, all that is understandable. It is your grandfather's character which has come out in you. And I shall tell you stories of all the travels he made when he was a young man, and then you will sleep. But first I must make my peace with your father.'

Outside, Ram Swarup finished smoking his *bidi,* and threw the stub away. From where it landed came a hiss. Ram Swarup was distraught: 'Nag Rajah, Nag Rajah, have I burnt you? Have I hit you?' Cautiously he approached the place where the stub had landed. Then he saw that it had fallen into the bowl of milk put out every evening by Amanti for the snake.

'Oh Ram, Ram,' he whispered. 'This is surely an evil omen. I must not tell my wife. But then again, she is renowned as an interpreter of such things. Perhaps I had better ask her.'

His wife put her head out of the door and called: 'Here, sulking husband, come back inside. You have frightened our daughter to tears with your talk of her marrying the Englishman. But what are you doing skulking down there? Gods, has he gone mad and is drinking the snake's milk?'

'No. Quiet. It is an omen, and you must interpret it.'

He told her what had happened. She stayed silent for what seemed ages to Ram Swarup, and held up her hands to prevent interruption.

'No,' she uttered finally with decision, 'it is a good omen. It means that the evil of uncontrolled passion will be extinguished by the milk of generosity.'

Ram Swarup laughed and grinned at his wife.

'You have fine teeth, my husband. They shine like eight silver rupees in the moonlight.'

And so they went inside, reconciled for the time being, and found that Amanti was smiling in her sleep.

Down at the palace, the Rajah and his wife had bid goodnight to their guests and retired to their room where they settled down to read for half an hour in bed, as was their custom. The Rani went back to *War and Peace*.

'Bolkonsky. . .' she started to say.

'You can say that again,' said the Rajah who had picked up coarse speech habits at the flight training centre in Middle Wallop.

'. . . is really my favourite character, though sometimes I believe I prefer Rostov.'

'They probably will,' said the Rajah picking up a paperback from the new pile arrived that morning. His wife looked at the title.

'*Escape from Stalag 13b?*' she queried. 'Isn't that scraping the barrel a bit?'

'There is no escape,' said the Rajah.

'What about the new Englishman?'

'Useless.'

'You mean he doesn't like it.'

'No. Sporting enough, mind you, but the intellectual type. Got on like a house on fire with those two downstairs.'

'Perhaps, dear, it is only big jets he dislikes. Many people hate them who are quite at ease in a smaller plane. Perhaps I should have a word with him. We might find a use for him. I have certain plans.'

'Just as you like. Anyway, one blessing, they leave tomorrow.'

They, being the Maharajah and his wife, stayed on out of ennui in the drawing room where the ancient and very deaf old Rani was entertaining them.

'I wish you would try to help poor Percy,' squeaked the old Rani. 'Did you know that your cousin-brother's uncle's mother's first wife, was third cousin to his grandfather's cousin-brother's auntie Bibbles?'

'Anguish,' groaned the Maharajah smiling beautifully at the old woman.

37

'That is so,' continued the old woman. 'Percy's wife is a dear, but. . .' and she held up a finger, looked around and leaned forward to whisper, 'she reads Russian books.'

She said the words 'Russian books' as a proud housewife might confide that she had discovered in her larder 'mice droppings'. She continued: 'It is unhealthy. Mr Hill might get to know and be forced to report her as a spy. There may be troop movements into the Khyber.'

'Who is Mr Hill?' whispered the Maharani to her husband.

'The last British resident. He left in '46. The British left years ago, you old fool!' he added to the old Rani.

'Oh don't be cross with her,' said the Maharani. 'I think she's absolutely marvellous. A new Englishman has come to the fort, great grandmother.'

'What's that, what did you say?'

'There are Englishmen in the fort!' he shouted in her ear.

'Mercy me!' cried the old woman. 'They have found out about her. I knew it. They will take Percy away for questioning. That I should live to see it. Bar the doors, call out the militia. We must escape in disguise. If only you could help poor Percy.'

'No, no,' said the Maharani, 'it is just one English school teacher. Would you like to meet him?'

'Certainly not. Send for Mr Hill. He is the only Englishman I will see. He will listen to me.'

The Maharajah called a servant and spoke with him.

'All the English have gone away again!' shouted the Maharajah in her ear.

'Safe. At least for the moment. My poor grandfather. . .' she drifted off into vague mumblings, then brightened up to say: 'Your dear daughter is so much like your poor dear wife. You really must marry again.'

'I have married again. This is my wife.'

'Yes, I agree, you should.'

'We must definitely ask the Englishman for the holidays,' said the Maharani. 'Even though you may have to be away.'

When all was quiet on the fort, and Ram Swarup had gone to bed, Arun Sen came out of his quarters and made his way towards the Junior School. His destination was a disused single storey building, occupied from time to time by male teachers at the Junior School; people who did not stay long. There he had agreed to meet Miss Willcox at one in the morning. When he came to the door, he whispered, 'Sheila, it's me.' When he received no answer, he carefully opened the door and went inside.

In the middle of the room was an oval table on which stood a green vase. If the vase were moved to the edge of the table, that signified she could not come. But the vase was in the centre of the table, and so he remained.

When half an hour had elapsed after the time for their meeting, he began to walk round the table rapping it repeatedly with his knuckles. After a further five minutes, he went outside and looked up at her window. There was no light in her room. He went back inside and waited a further ten minutes. Then he took up the vase, and uttering a curse, flung it hard against the wall where it shattered into many pieces.

6

During Priestman's first few days at the school, many boys came to his rooms in the evening. Most were in a panic about public examinations; others came out of curiosity or just for a change. Priestman enjoyed their visits. He was flattered and helpful.

By the middle of the first week, apart from half a dozen exam worriers, only one boy paid regular social calls. Ashok was fourteen and awkward. He had the slightly puffy cheeks and glazed eyes of someone finding puberty difficult. Most of the time, he roamed about the room casually picking up objects and putting them down somewhere else as though he were dissatisfied with the entire arrangement of the place. He held in contempt the boys who came for extra tuition.

'They expect you to work magic for them, sir. They think that just by sitting next to you they will get the answers. They have not worked and now they are panicking.'

'And you, Ashok? Are you working now so you won't have to panic next year?'

'No sir. I am simply panicking now very calmly one year in advance.'

'And that is why you are always darting round the room?'

'No sir, just restless. We live just for cycle trips out, sir. Will you take us on a cycle trip?'

'Of course.'

'Marvellous. We could go to Mander Pan where Mr Arun Sen took us on a trip last year, and where he was very frightened by a report from a man there that a tiger had been seen only three weeks before we arrived. So he told us all to ride back, and we never saw the place properly. Or we could go to the beautiful Birta lake. Beside it is the old Rajah's hunting lodge which is shaped like a bi-plane. It's empty now, but so strange and beautiful.'

'Really! So you're interested in architecture?'

'I am interested in thousands of things, sir.'

It seemed to Priestman that here was a child that would be almost impossible to teach in the conventional sense; knowledge or something like it was inherent in him. He was not concerned with pupil/teacher relationships or with Indian/English relationships, or anything of that kind. Priestman wondered how he could speak to him without adopting some strained attitude. He seemed to want some sort of relationship, to be demanding something more than a bicycle trip.

'So you will take us for a cycle trip on Sunday, sir?'

'I'm sorry, Ashok, I can't this Sunday. There's an annual fete at some village sponsored by the school. Bhonsa or something. I have to go.'

'Really boring, sir.'

'So everyone keeps telling me.'

'It's a rich village, though they pretend they are really poor. All money from the school goes straight into the pockets of the headman and his friends. Even the outcastes who serve the headman go around in English suits on festival days. Don't go, sir.'

'I have to. And anyway it will be my first trip into the Indian countryside, and my first real look at an Indian village at close quarters. I might even slip away into the jungle.'

'It's just broken up rough country, hardly any trees. You might see a few porcupines, or find some poor little village whose people really need the money. And there is a madman there, sir. A mad beggar. A magician, sir. He is famed all around this area for curing snake bites. People really believe in his powers. You must give him some money.' Priestman laughed. 'Don't laugh, sir. These people have great power in India. It is better not to laugh at them. If he comes up, give him some money and go away quickly. Now I must go sir. So the Sunday after, O.K, sir?'

'I'm not sure. I'll let you know.'

'Fine, sir. Thank you, sir. Goodnight, sir.'

When Ashok had left, Edward had time to pay attention to the fact that he no longer enjoyed the taste of cigarettes. He kept

41

running his tongue over his teeth, and salivating to get rid of an unpleasant taste. His vision seemed slightly impaired so that he was constantly blinking. Then pains started in his stomach, and he became unsteady on his feet.

In the middle of the night, he awoke and lay for a long time hoping the feeling of nausea and the desire to vomit would pass. But it did not, and the rest of the night he spent in the bathroom. Next day he had to keep to his rooms.

At midday, the principal, Banglaratnam and the English department visited his sick bed and acted as though they had inadvertently poisoned him. The nurse was called. She brought some medicine which the others looked at suspiciously, while asking frowning questions of her. Once the principal had assured himself that Priestman had nothing seriously wrong with him, he left, saying that as soon as Priestman was better, he should call on the Rajah.

'Edward, this is terrible, terrible!' cried Banglaratnam.

Although Edward was exhausted, he had got over the worst and was actually feeling quite hungry as well as cheerful. So he laughed at the vice-principal's exaggeration, and winked at Panwar. The vice-principal was infected by the laughter.

'It is really amazing,' he said. 'How can you laugh? This is bravery.' And he laughed as well.

'Oh, I'll be up and around tomorrow; it's only a tummy bug.'

'How can you think of such a thing? Only a tummy bug. What bug? What bug, nurse?'

'There is some vomiting and loose motions,' she answered laconically, eyeing the patient, who frowned at this public exposure of his condition.

'It could be anything,' continued Banglaratnam. 'And his temperature?'

'It is a little above normal,' said the nurse.

'How much?'

'A degree or so.'

'Is it coming down or going up?'

'Coming down.'

'Coming down. That is a good sign. It will not come down too far, nurse?'

'It will probably come down to normal.'

'Too low a temperature is as bad as too high.'

'More dangerous,' said the nurse.

'Much more dangerous!' exclaimed Banglaratnam. 'What are you giving him?'

The nurse muttered something unintelligible which sounded like 'something of something'. Priestman felt that it was time he too contributed to the conversation.

'The patient is as good as cured by all this wonderful attention and concern.'

Everybody seemed very pleased with this statement which Edward considered must have approximated to some polite Hindi formula for such occasions. Only the nurse let her smile fade quickly. She was standing back from the bedside, composed and aloof, but her eyes were fixed on his half-exposed curly haired chest. Priestman caught and held her gaze for a moment, but since she did not turn her eyes away, he sighed slightly, and feeling of a sudden exhausted, looked up at the ceiling, and hoped that his visitors would go.

Except for occasional exclamations, Arun Sen and Panwar had remained silent, which puzzled Priestman. He considered that it must be the presence of the nurse that was inhibiting them rather than that of their superior. But then it came to him that he too was their superior, and that therefore a certain formality from them was probably due to him in public.

Banglaratnam began to discourse poetically on the model dairy herd attached to Throgton School in Cheshire. Enormous cows had loomed out of the mist at him ten years ago and at this time of year. The longing which this kind old man felt for England began to infect Priestman.

'Come now, Mr Banglaratnam, you must not make me home-sick as well as tummy sick.'

Banglaratnam laughed, but he seemed near to tears at his own rememberings. 'You will call again in the evening, nurse, to ascertain his general condition and take his temperature.'

'No need for that,' said Priestman. 'I shall be up and dashing around by then. Well, I shall be up, anyway.'

'He will be dashing about quietly in his chair,' said Panwar.

Banglaratnam shook his head from side to side as though pondering something, then suddenly brightened up and flapping one hand, left crying out, 'Marvellous! Marvellous! Come. We must not tire him.' And so they all left.

During afternoon school, Arun Sen, who had two free periods, came alone to visit Priestman.

'I am so glad that we are alone at last,' said Arun. 'I was worried that those others were boring and tiring you.'

'Tell me something about the people at this school, Arun.' Priestman had taken a very light lunch of boiled vegetables, and had had to creep back to bed feeling far weaker than he had supposed. He really wanted to sleep.

'Ah, now Panwar,' began Arun. 'Don't misunderstand me; he is my friend. We share the same quarters. But really, he must be very careful or he will get into the most awful trouble.'

'Whatever do you mean?'

'Well, you know the play *Macbeth*. He became terribly involved in it, emotionally, I mean.'

'All to the good. It was splendid.'

'Oh, yes, very good. It is just that he was a little free with some of his emotions where some of the cast were concerned.'

'You mean that he clipped the Porter round the ear for not knowing his lines?'

'Ha, ha! You are always so witty, Edward. No, the boys become very emotional at these times, particularly those with major parts, and it was necessary to spend long hours alone with some of them, coaching them in their lines, etc.'

'Well, I suppose that you are trying to tell me something bad about him. You mean he had a homosexual affair with Lady Macbeth or one of the witches?'

'Really, how quick are you, Edward. But you are going too fast for me, jumping ahead too much. I do not say there was anything physical in it; more platonic perhaps, but definitely a very strong emotional involvement. So we must be discreet for his sake.'

'Talking about it like this hardly seems discreet. Don't think me offended, but I'm not one for gossip. If you have proof that he physically had an affair with one of the boys, then it is your duty to ask him for his version, and if you are still not satisfied, to tell him that he should resign or else you will have to take the matter up with the principal.'

'Of course, you are absolutely right, but I would do nothing to harm him. He is my friend. I simply thought that you would like to know, that you should know.'

'Well, since there seems nothing to know, then I don't.' Priestman looked at the wall, hoping that his visitor would take the hint and go.

'Oh, I see that you are angry with me,' cried Arun Sen, smiling and raising his hands as though in distress. 'Forgive me for saying so, but you are so new here. You cannot understand the way everybody gossips. It is all so regrettable, I agree. But it is such an isolated place. I will give you an example. That mathematics master, Mattacharya, who runs the Hindi section of the School Review, is really dangerous. He does not like the English department at all. He doesn't like the English language either. Every night you will see him going to the principal's bungalow, bearing tittle-tattle of every sort. So, others too must go and put their point of view to the principal, otherwise they will be out on their ears in no time at all. Now, the housemaster and geography teacher, Patel, I tell you. . .'

'Enough. This is terrible, and I have no intention of taking part in any of it.'

'Of course not. Anyway, you as an Englishman are in no way affected by all this. Everybody is most fond of you. I am simply warning you that if, for example, you should want a little flirtation, and I do not suggest of course that you do, then you must be ever so discreet. Miss Willcox of the Junior School, now she is not discreet. It would be not at all wise.'

'Well, I had no intention of it. I don't even know who she is.'

'Oh, you will meet her. She and others like her will make it their business to meet you before long. Those women have the reputation of not being very nice girls, and particularly Miss Willcox. It is said that she may not be very clean.'

'You mean she doesn't wash often enough?'

'Edward, what a marvellous sense of humour you have. No. I mean not very clean in other ways.'

'Oh! I see. Anyway, it doesn't concern me. Let's just say that I had enough of women in England, and that I am here to get away from them all, and to do a job of work.'

'How very stern you are, Edward. How British. We poor

Indians are so much more emotional.'

'Rubbish!'

'Ha, ha! That is becoming your favourite word for what I say. You are very severe on me! Of course, the nurse you know is very available. And I have it on good authority that she is very clean and discreet. Nurses you know are low creatures in this country, not like your nurses. Your predecessor, for example, was very attached to her. It was an open secret. Of course, being a nurse, it did not matter. And since he was an Englishman and so cut off from his own people, it was accepted that it was a good arrangement for him. Nobody minded, and it was all kept sort of hush-hush.'

'Very, by the sound of it. I thought you said she was discreet.'

'Oh, she would be willing to be very discreet. It was Macgregor who was not discreet. He did not give a damn towards the end for anybody.'

'Did you know him well?'

'Oh yes. We were great friends. We had many marvellous chats here in this very room. But at the end, he became not very nice to people. He was rather abusive, particularly to his department. He thought he was some sort of old-fashioned imperial *pukka sahib* lording it over the natives.'

'How appalling.'

'Yes. And do you know that he actually kicked me. Mind you he was drunk, so I forgave him straight away. We were great friends. But that is why we are all so frightened of you Edward, and say the wrong things.'

'Oh, for heaven's sake, do I act like a *pukka sahib*?'

'Of course not. You are a really modern Englishman. And I just thought you should know about the nurse in case you wished me to make some arrangement.'

'It sounds a perfectly appalling arrangement to me. Anyway, I have no intention of walking into my predecessor's shoes, if that is the right expression. So thanks for coming to see me. I'm a bit tired now. And don't conclude from what I've said that I'm a prude or something. I'm really grateful for our little chat. And do come and see me again when I'm feeling better, and we'll have a good laugh. Oh yes. One thing you might be able to help me with; the principal said that I should call on the Rajah. Today's

46

Thursday, so I suppose I had better go Saturday afternoon. But tell me, this calling business sounds very old-fashioned. I assume that I am supposed to go and leave my card, and I haven't got a card, of course. So what's the form?'

'Oh, just go down there, and present yourself, and some aide or other will tell them that you are there.'

When Arun Sen had left, Priestman felt hot after being in bed for so long in the dark, stuffy little room. He opened the bedroom shutters but the sudden blinding light and the incessant *kark, kark, kark* of the crows forced him to close the shutters again. He returned wearily to bed. *Check, check, check* went a gecko near the ceiling. Priestman threw a sandal at it, but his aim was poor. *Check, check, check* responded the gecko louder. 'So,' thought Priestman, 'one can't shut India out because it's already inside.'

Later in the day, the shouting of the boys returning from class woke Priestman. Panwar came in. They talked desultorily for a while until Edward said that he was really too tired to talk.

'You know,' said Edward, 'I'm sorry I'm such a bad host. Why don't you tell me something about Indian literature. I'm afraid I'm really very ignorant about it. Perhaps you could make a list of books I should read.'

'The *Ramayana* you have of course read,' said Panwar. Edward confessed that he had not.

'It is our most famous epic.'

'What is it about?' asked Edward a trifle wearily.

'Rama, son of king Dasa-Ratha, married Sita who was born miraculously from a field furrow. . .'

'Ah.'

'After the marriage, Dasa-Ratha. . .'

'Who's he again?'

'Rama's father. He said that he would abdicate and let Rama rule in his place. But he was tricked by his young wife into giving the throne to her son instead of to Rama. So Rama was sent into exile with Sita and his brother Laksman. They crossed many rivers including the Ganges, and plunged deep into the forest. There they met a saint who encouraged them to make a dwelling in the forest of Panchwah. But a Raksha princess. . .'

'A what?'

'A sort of devil, fell in love with Rama, and tried to destroy Sita. But Laksman split her nose and ears with his sword.'

'Jolly good!'

'She complained to Ravana, the devil king of Ceylon, and to Marisha who disguised herself as a doe in order to trick Sita. So Ravana carried off Sita by force, and. . . You are asleep, Edward, I think.'

Panwar left quietly, making sure that the netting door did not bang as he went out.

7

While Edward slept, Ram Swarup's wife prepared their evening meal with the help of Amanti. Ram Swarup ran his tongue over his lips at the smell of linseed and sesame oil. He watched with pleasure Amanti's hands silhouetted, in the gloomy hut, against the fire light as she kneaded the dough for bread, pressing her hands deep into the mass, soggy with buffalo milk, squeezing it with her clever fingers, then slapping and rolling it into balls between her palms.

'So,' said his wife, 'your Englishman has already succumbed to the nurse's witchcraft.' She passed the mortar to Amanti to continue grinding, and straightened up. 'Why must you smoke that filthy *bidi* in here and poison us all? As if there is not smoke enough.' She wiped her hands, and took down a leaf from a bunch hanging near the door. 'You smoke much more now that you have become so rich.'

'The English are strong,' said Ram Swarup calmly. 'You do not remember the old English principal. He survived all sorts of illnesses and witchcraft. My father, you know, served him.'

'Yes, you have told me many times. That Englishman sat crosslegged, wore a *dhoti* and turban, and pretended that he was a brahmin. Yet he smoked an English pipe. What foolishness! Well, what of him?'

'The Rajah likes to have an Englishman as principal of his school, and our present Indian principal is past retiring age.' Ram Swarup prepared a silence to let this information sink in. But his wife broke it almost immediately.

'So when will you travel to see your barber's man?'

'We have no need of the barber. The leader of the Bhonsa sweepers is a rich man. It is a rich village. He has a son.' Amanti

49

pounded harder in the mortar, so that her mother told her that she had ground the ingredients enough.

'Bhonsa is it! Bhonsa is only half a day's ride by bullock cart from here. Would you have our daughter marry a relative?'

'Would you have me journey to the moon for a husband, you irritating woman?'

'I thought you had been there already, you watch it so often with such longing.'

'Why do I bother to talk to you?'

'Well, well, and what of this Bhonsa man?'

'I have made enquiries. There seems no immediate bar to it. But I must find out more.'

'When will you find our more?'

'There is to be the sports fete at Bhonsa on Sunday. Edward Sahib, the principal, everybody will be there. I shall set off on foot before dawn. Choti Lal and Bhagat Chand will go with me.'

'And this man, how rich is he?'

'The village headman is his master. For ten generations it has been so. He has his own house, a bicycle and wears an English suit on festival days.'

'Oh, goddess Lakshmi, is he an Englishman too? Would you have your daughter marry a millionaire? We shall be ruined. You will have to give a new suit and a bicycle to the boy and a hundred rupees. Now I will stir,' she continued, taking the spoon from Amanti. Crouching over the pot, she began to stir, and the rhythm of her movements gave to her utterances the quality of a chant. 'The groom's father will have ten singers. He will have two bands at the wedding. He will give twelve ornaments for your daughter's feet. He will give six for her neck. He will give four for her hands. He will give mountains of *ghi* and twenty *maunds* of wheat.' She flung down the spoon and began to pace round the little room. Ram Swarup watched her in growing despair. But Amanti could scarcely control her laughter, for her mother had simply doubled the normal number for these gifts among the rich.

'Oh Ram, Ram, preserve me! What do you want, woman? Do you want a squint-eyed idiot for a son-in-law?'

His wife squatted down again by the pot, took the spoon from Amanti, and sipped the contents. She nodded to Amanti, who

50

added something to the brew from a tin, and took the spoon from her mother.

'And you, foolish man, will have to give more than the groom's father, as tradition demands.' She watched Amanti stirring, and nodded at each turn of the spoon. 'The groom's party will be a thousand men.' Amanti laughed outright. 'There!' continued Ram Swarup's wife, 'see how your daughter bravely chokes back her tears at the absurdity of your monstrous ambition. And the dowry? Your worthless brother will not be able to help. He will hardly know what to do with the boy at the oil bath ceremony. And the dresses and money you must give your daughter, and. . . alright, man, run away outside and spit under the moon. Perhaps you will find the money where your spit lands.'

Ram Swarup stood angrily in the doorway.

'In that case, I shall not go to Bhonsa on Sunday. I am going now to tell Choti Lal and Bhagat Chand that the trip will not take place.'

'What a temper the man has. You can say nothing to him but he flies into a rage. Did I say you should not go?' The wife smiled, and Amanti began to serve the food.

'And while you were at it,' grumbled Ram Swarup, coming back into the room and squatting down to receive his bowl, 'you did not mention the nose ornament.'

'First it is drunken Englishmen and barbers he frightens me with. Then he insults me about my teeth and skin. Now he threatens me with a naked nose in the family, a nose which is a disgrace to our ancestors and to all generations to come. Where will it all end, I ask the gods?'

'But my naked nose can smell the smell of newly-baked bread, which nobody can make like our daughter,' said Ram Swarup, helping himself to a hot chapatti from the pile.

That night, Amanti dreamed that she was naked and riding an enormous shiny bicycle. It ran away with her into the water tank where she had bathed with the boys when the monsoon rains broke. And she dreamed that it was the new Englishman who dragged her out.

Meanwhile, the new Englishman, feeling much better after his sleep, declined the proferred 'English meal' of soggy boiled

51

vegetables, and ate with relish a meat curry with chapattis, rice, *dhal*, pickle and finished with a rather disappointing little brown fruit with papery flesh. Though he sweated profusely at the spiciness of it all, he was well satisfied, his only regret being that he lacked a bottle of red wine. He ate on the central table of the living room, already forming a home for his books and papers, which having remained undisturbed since the day before, had acquired an aggressive air of territorial right. 'Home is where the book is,' said Priestman to the room. 'It would be good to listen to some of my Bach records, or perhaps Mozart would be better for the digestion. It has been a Wagnerian experience, forsooth. No, I am in a First Brandenburg Concerto mood – rousing without pomp, full of promise of splendid things to come, and suffused with good health and humour. Pom, pom, pom, pom, pom, pom, poppadum,' he hummed.

'And is that not like my life at the moment? Everything is full of promise. I am invited by beautiful maharanis to ski or whatever in the hills with them. I am invited to plunge into tropical Bengal on the trail of an unknown fearsome carnivore. I am bidden to fly south on the scent of magnificent cheeses. I am bidden to call upon rajahs in their palaces. I am to be chief guest at the sports on Sunday. I am liked. I am a success. India is not my oyster; it is my large and lovely pearl through and around which I may cruise, caressed at little expense.

'Furthermore, now is the time ripe once again for the Englishman to continue his long search for this lost land.' Priestman began to pace the room, gesticulating and muttering. 'Yes, a search so rudely interrupted by the arrival here in the middle of the last century of the English wife, who dragged me away from my Indian mistresses. With them I placed my finger upon the throbbing pulse of bazaar, court and village. But she dragged me back, scrubbed behind my ears, and set me down grumpy before a bowl of boiled cabbage in a stuffy brick copy of Daddy's house in Hove or Halifax. Why! The Indian Mutiny would not have occurred without her interference.

'Now all that is over, you boiled-water flint-gun carrying, joint-account British woman, red in tooth and nose. Now once again, free after a hundred years of colonization by the British woman – and it was hard, my Indian friends, for all of us – I shall go forth. . .'

There was a soft tap on the door. When Priestman saw the nurse, whose proposed visit he had forgotten, he was irritated. He and the room were not yet ready to receive any woman. He indicated a chair, and seated himself opposite her. Her eyes seemed veiled and blurred, and the iris was yellow round the edges. He could not decide whether her languid movements and the sallowness of her complexion were the marks of a 'type' or of a past illness. Had Macgregor beaten her too, he wondered.

'How are you feeling?' she asked without apparent interest.

'Oh, I'm fine. Nothing wrong with me at all.'

'You must be careful. You must not take our illnesses too lightly. I should take your temperature.'

'There's no need. I know it's normal.'

She did not insist, and was quiet. A long pause ensued; to him embarrassing.

'Have you a radio?' she asked.

'No I haven't.' He was irritated by his inability to entertain her. 'I have brought some records, but the record player was too heavy to bring on the plane.' She blinked, probably, thought Edward, not understanding about aircraft baggage allowances. 'I'm afraid I can't even offer you a drink, I mean whisky or something. When I'm properly organized we can have a party. I gather you and Arun Sen know some of the women teachers from the Junior School. Perhaps they would come along.'

'They would not come. They do not have anything to do with Senior School. We do not have drinking parties here like you do in England. Though I occasionally take a little light brandy, particularly in wintertime. If we do drink, it is quietly behind doors. It is necessary to be discreet.' She looked down and adjusted the folds of her sari.

'I could offer you some coffee, of course.'

'No, thank you. Mr Macgregor had a radio.'

'I see. Well, I don't really feel the need of one. When I do, then I shall buy one.'

'My home is in Bombay. I shall be in Bombay during the holidays. Will you go to Bombay in the holidays? You should go. It is the most modern city in India. It is not like here. You would be more at home there.'

53

'I'm not sure where I'm going yet in the holidays. They're still six or seven weeks away.'

'My family would be pleased to welcome you in Bombay. So you will tell me when you are coming, and I will give you my address.'

'That's very kind. I shall let you know as soon as I can.'

'There is no hurry. Have you had bowel motions today?'

He replied frowning that he had not, and that he considered it a very good thing.

'We Indians are not ashamed of our natural functions,' continued the nurse. 'And now I must go.' She remained seated, however, looking directly at him.

'It was kind of you to come,' said Priestman getting up and going to the door.

He let her out. Making no reply to his 'goodnight', she slipped quickly past him, and to his surprise, made off with much greater speed than he had thought her capable of.

Because Priestman had slept so much during the day, he now felt alert and restless. He decided to go for a walk, and still wearing only pyjamas and dressing-gown, made for the old cannon and the battlements. At the cannon he met Ashok and another boy who was not wearing the regulation evening wear of *kurta*-pyjamas.

'Ashok, you should have been in bed hours ago. It's half past eleven.'

'I was restless, sir.'

'Well, go to bed now. Who's your friend?'

'One of the servant boys, sir. A very low caste fellow, sir. Really untouchable.' Ashok put his arm round the other boy's shoulders, and they both grinned. 'He is a great hunter, sir. He found two leopard cubs and brought them to my home.'

'That's wonderful. Your friend lives in the jungle.'

'Oh yes, sir. He is a very savage fellow. A real tribal. He is the son of my uncle's *shikari*. For many days, my friend and I track animals and watch them.'

'Do you shoot them?'

'No, no. We just watch.'

'And do you write down your observations?'

'No. That is biology, sir. We do not do biology class in the jungle. My friend has lived in the jungle all his life. He knows the names of all plants, animals and insects, and where they are found and why. But he does not read or write yet. He is terribly untouchable and bites, sir.' He said something to the boy in Hindi, and the boy replied with a growl. 'Mowgli, sir. Wolf boy. But now I am teaching him to read. Why should I be taught to read and not him? And he is really quick, sir. Not like some of these fat city boys from Bombay or Calcutta. Some of them are really dumb. They spend all the holidays in air-conditioned cinemas seeing the same American film ten times over. They go walking around pretending they are cowboys with sore behinds.'

Priestman laughed. 'But I thought you weren't allowed to have anything to do with outcastes.'

'That is all nonsense, sir. "I am a brahmin, you are this, he is that." All stupid talk by boring people. You should see some of these boys at their homes, sir. If a fly comes and settles on their nose, they call a servant to come and chase it off. This fellow and I have eaten from the same bowl since we were babies, sir.'

'But what do your parents think about that?'

'My uncle thinks the same as I do, sir. He is very angry with people who try to keep up this nonsense.'

'I see. But what is your friend doing here?'

'He was lonely without me, sir. So he ran a hundred and fifty miles to join me. But that is nothing for him. He lopes along like a wolf, sir.' Once again Ashok said something to the boy, who grinned and trotted round and round the cannon then over to the battlements and back. 'And now we must go, sir.'

When they had gone, Priestman ran his hand over the cannon, then tried to push its barrel. But the cannon did not budge even a fraction of an inch.

He walked to the ruined battlements, and as he looked over, a dull roar came up to him. He stepped back experimentally and the sound stopped. Moving forward again and looking over, he realized that it was the sound of hundreds of voices, of singing and the playing of instruments in the town below. The smell of cooking, and of charcoal fires was wafted up to him. From time to time as the wind changed, came the individual cries of people and the barking of dogs – all very clear as though they were much nearer. And the background to all this sound was the beating of many drums. Beyond the town, the still large but waning moon sat on a far hill illuminating the white domes of the Rajah's palace, and beyond, though Priestman did not know what they were, a few lights winked like miniature lighthouses, beckoning from the village of Bhonsa.

As he walked back, Priestman started to hum the opening bars of the First Brandenburg Concerto. But he soon stopped humming. The music now seemed to him trite, and to have lost its assurance in the face of the vast night sky which throbbed with more stars than he had ever seen.

8

Despite his colleagues' protests, Priestman took classes the next day. At lunchtime, he found awaiting him a very sealed and be-crested envelope containing a friendly letter from the Maharani inviting him to spend a week after Christmas at her winter resort in the mountains.

When afternoon school was over, Ram Swarup came to Priestman's rooms, and picking up Priestman's camera indicated that he would like a photograph taken of himself. Priestman readily agreed. Ram Swarup then hurried off to his own quarters while Priestman wandered around on the verandah and in the garden focussing the camera and testing the light. When Ram Swarup came back with Amanti rather reluctantly in tow, Priestman was somewhat surprised. He recognized her as the girl he had noticed the first day and subsequently by the water tap, but had never connected her with his servant.

'No, not there,' said Priestman. 'We want to get the sun coming in from the side.' He took several shots of them together just outside the verandah. Then Ram Swarup indicated that he wanted Amanti taken by herself.

Priestman waved his arms to indicate where she should stand, and she obeyed his instructions rather wistfully and with a rueful smile. By now, several children and servants had gathered to watch and make remarks. Priestman kept them quiet by taking the occasional shot of them, at which they would stiffen up and pose horribly, save one little boy dressed only in a shirt, and too young to understand. He came up to Priestman and stared at him hand in mouth. Then a woman shouted from the servants' quarters, and the child began to run around getting in Priestman's way until Amanti picked him up, and speaking quietly to him, carried him away on her hip a little distance. Then he freed himself and scuttled back to the servants' quarters.

The crows, squirrels and parrots were annoyed by all this activity, and doubled the volume of their usual harsh cries. And as they did so the cries of the women increased. They kept out of sight or some way off, their faces partially covered. Nevertheless it seemed they controlled the proceedings.

Finally, Priestman had Amanti pose leaning against the tree. She put one foot against the trunk as though about to climb it, and looked at Priestman enquiringly. The servants laughed. 'So, you have a sense of humour as well as beauty, have you?' thought Priestman.

'When do you want them?' Priestman asked the beaming Ram Swarup. 'When photographs?'

'Bhonsa,' said Ram Swarup holding up three fingers.

'That's a rush. Three days.' He wrote the following note: 'Please process express one roll black and white film, two sets of contacts. Show bearer contacts and print up to six one-off 8 x 6 inch to his choice.' Then he gave the note and twenty rupees to Ram Swarup, while Amanti, holding a square can, stood beside the tap waiting for the water supply to come on. Priestman was irritated that he had not thought of taking her photograph in that pose, though she would, of course, have had to borrow a traditional earthenware pot, and not use that ugly tin.

That night Priestman read late under the mosquito net. Through the wire netting of the open window he could see occasional flashes of lightning far off. He put the book down on the bedside table, turned off the light, and lay on his back. Then he saw something strange out of the corner of his eye. As he turned, he saw the head of a cobra, with hood extended, swaying towards him and away, not twelve inches from his face.

'Don't move a muscle,' he thought, 'it may go away.' He waited. The swaying continued. He cursed inwardly that he had left the hockey stick, kept for such emergencies, just inside the bathroom doorway, having been told that if a snake were to come, it would be most likely to do so via the waste water channel leading from the bath.

He considered whether, if the snake struck, the mosquito net would give him any protection. He doubted it; the material was too flimsy and was slack. Then he began slowly to edge the hand farthest from the snake and on the living room door side under the netting. Gently he eased some of the netting out, eyes never leaving the head of the snake. Sometimes the head seemed to draw back and pause as though to strike, and he held his breath, his far hand gripping the edge of the mattress. But when the snake started to sway again, Priestman continued to ease the netting out until he considered there was sufficient gap for him to make a rapid exit. He tightened his lips at the thought that he had shut the communicating door between bedroom and living room.

Priestman did not know whether he made any decision to act, but suddenly he was out from under the net and at the door thrusting aside its bolt, and expecting any moment to feel the blow and stab of fangs in his naked heel. With one hand he flung open the door while with the other he grabbed the hockey stick. It trailed behind him and became stuck in the door as he tried to shut it from the living room side. Furiously wriggling the stick, he managed to get it out and slam the door shut. He paused for a moment to catch his breath, but then realizing there was room for a snake to get under the door, he made a dash for his front door and went outside.

Patel of the geography department was the housemaster of the adjoining buildings. There was a light in his room. Priestman went in.

'Good evening Mr Patel. I'm sorry to disturb you so late.'
Patel rose, smiling in a puzzled way at his dishevelled visitor, hair awry and clad only in pyjamas.

'The trouble is that I'm afraid I seem to have a snake in my bedroom and I'm not really very experienced at dealing with them. Perhaps you could tell me how to go about it. A large cobra, I should think.' Priestman joined and extended his palms to indicate the hood.

Patel instantly made for the door shouting in Hindi. In a very short time, six or eight servants including Ram Swarup, had gathered. They carried sticks and were shod with old army or football boots. They followed Patel and Priestman to his rooms. Priestman slightly opened the bedroom door, and the men approached cautiously, sticks raised. Then Priestman got a hand through the door, and switched on the light. The shape beside the bed had gone. Emboldened and heedless of Patel's warnings to let the men deal with it, Priestman led the little group forward. They fanned out, poking their sticks into corners and under the bed. But nothing could they find.

Then it seemed to occur to them all at the same time that the snake had fled to the bathroom. Priestman once again led them in. They banged the chest of drawers, poked behind the lavatory, and rained blows on the side of the bath. Priestman pointed out the open drain. The men nodded and chattered, evidently convincing themselves that the snake had escaped through the channel by which it had presumably entered. Priestman wondered why nobody had considered putting some netting over the drain. He vowed that he would have it done the next day.

'It will not come back tonight,' Patel assured Priestman.

'You mean he was more frightened than me?' laughed Priestman. They all laughed at a danger receded if not overcome, and left with Priestman's apologies for disturbing them.

Alone, he lit a cigarette and made some coffee, unwilling to return to the darkness and fear beneath the mosquito net. After half an hour, he went back to bed, taking the hockey stick with him. Reaching under the net, he turned off the bedside lamp. Within a few seconds, the snake was beside him again, swaying and ready to strike.

'This is impossible!' shouted Priestman at the snake. 'You're not there, and if you are you've had it!' He grabbed the hockey stick and struck out at the object, then immediately jumped out of bed and switched on the main light. Nothing. Cautiously he edged round the bed, stick at the ready.

Then he saw the 'snake'. As the breeze coming through the window stiffened, a piece of scrap paper he had torn to act as a book marker was raised vertically, then slowly subsided as the breeze slackened. Its shape, even in the bright light, was remarkably like that of a cobra's hood. He ripped the paper out of the book, and crumpled it up. He would have some explaining to do in the morning. But he considered that this example of human fallibility would be no bad thing in his case, since it would counteract the role of hero recently given him, and not everyone wishes to live alongside a hero.

Next morning at break in the staff room, there was a bated-breath expectancy among the teachers to hear about the snake episode. As they poured out and handed one another the milky tea, Arun Sen began: 'We hear, Edward, that you had an experience last night.'

'Enormous cobra,' said Patel, 'fast, too, by the way it vanished. Edward was in the forefront with a hockey stick. I held him back in vain.'

The vice-principal bustled in agog.

'Two inches from my nose,' said Priestman. 'Tell me, if it had struck, would the mosquito net have afforded any protection?'

There followed a lengthy discussion about quality of netting material, angle and force of strike, sex and age of snake, time of year, etc.

'The most boring thing, Mr Patel,' continued Priestman, 'is that after you left, it came back.'

Priestman's audience fell silent.

'But you are unbitten,' cried Arun Sen, his tongue darting over his lips.

'By all appearances, he is totally unbitten,' said Panwar.

'Please tell us,' cried Banglaratnam, 'that you are totally unbitten. We beg you!'

'As far as he is able to ascertain,' said Priestman, 'the patient remains unbitten. Though if a paper book marker could bite, he would stand before you well and thoroughly bitten.' Priestman then explained, and the joy and laughter among the staff was unbounded. Some things are supposed to make a person's day. This episode seemed to make the staff's term. The bell rang for class, and as the others went out, Banglaratnam came up to Priestman. It seemed that somehow it had lodged in his mind that Priestman had been subject to some attack.

'Nevertheless,' he said looking serious, 'there is known to be a large cobra in that area. Something must be done to get rid of it. Yes, something must definitely be done. The principal is most distressed!' He left tutting and laughing by turns.

'Is that true?' asked Priestman of Panwar as they left for class.

'I hear that there is very probably such a snake.'

'Well, that's ridiculous. It could kill someone.'

'They say it does no harm. It is a god, you see. Besides, it kills rats.'

'Alright, alright, I know, it's holy, and somebody's grandfather. So, if it's so harmless, why doesn't somebody put it in a basket and dump it in the jungle?'

'They say it belongs to the place, and that the place belongs to it.'

'And what is its territory? How far does it roam?'

'Who knows?'

'Yes, well, in theory I approve of all that sort of thing, provided it occurs far away in the jungle. But on my doorstep is quite another matter.'

9

On the following Saturday afternoon, Miss Willcox received a note: 'Dear Sheila, I must have offended you. You are avoiding me. I am holding a small at home party for Edward Priestman who has expressed a desire to meet you. Since alcoholic beverages will be served, I thought it more discreet to hold the party at our little place, yours and mine (do you remember it?). It will be tonight at 8.00 p.m. sharp.

'Please forgive such short notice. I have so long been deliberating whether or not to invite you; you have for so long avoided me. Eventually, after much heart-searching, I concluded that it would be discourteous not to issue this invitation, particularly in view of the aforementioned circumstances. Moreover, you will be in company, and need not therefore speak to me if you do not wish it, save perhaps for a few civilities. Give no reply to the bearer of this note, and destroy it immediately by fire and thereafter stamp out the ashes. Yours faithfully, Arun Sen.'

When Miss Willcox arrived at 8.15, she found Arun Sen alone. Glasses were laid out on the central table. There were some bottles of whisky and gin on a dressing table, together with six large bottles of beer. There were pistachio nuts, peanuts and other delicacies on a tray.

'Is my watch wrong?' queried Miss Willcox coldly, looking round the room. 'It is normally such an excellent timepiece.'

'No, no. This is terrible,' said Arun Sen laughing. 'I have just had word that Priestman and all the others have been detained by the principal.'

'Sunita too?'

'Ah, your nurse friend is needed for some question of his health, I believe. Distressing. Perhaps you would care to come

63

back in a quarter of an hour.' She made no reply, but watched him closely. He mixed two large gins with orange juice, concentrating solely on the task, his tongue slightly between his teeth.

'You have overdone the perfume,' she said sitting down and accepting the drink. 'An Englishman will find it cloying. The whole place smells like a brothel.'

'Tush, how would you know? On the contrary, it smells like a palace, like the harem of a prince in days of old when all India was a palace, when all men were princes in the land, and all women like the goddesses, when lovers walked unashamed naked through the land. When India was like the temples of Khajuraho. Then, you Sheila Willcox would have taken pride in your womanhood. You would not have borne an English name nor an English cross around your neck. See, look at the new book of the temples I have bought.' He picked up a large art book from the central table, and brought it to the couch where he seated himself beside her. He started to turn the pages, she silently watching him, not the book. 'And you, I have often wondered while turning these pages alone the last few days, which of these naked goddesses you most resemble.' He laughed and began to sing in a low, pleasant voice, sometimes humming and rocking slightly as he turned the pages. 'Is it the goddess Parvati here who stands so proudly with Siva, his hand supporting her breast?' He whistled the tune under his breath, tapping his fingers against his glass.

'No, this is not right,' said Miss Willcox jumping up. 'They will be here any minute.'

'They will not come till nine,' said Arun remaining seated. 'I deceived you for love. Forgive me.' He stood up and went to a cupboard. 'But to show how contrite I am, receive these poor presents of mine. Sit, sit. There is no harm.' He returned with a brown paper parcel, and stood beside the couch smiling at her.

'I vowed in church never to see you again.' Her voice was more hesitant now, but she still stood near the door, eyeing the parcel.

'Ah, then you are not to blame. Your Christian god talking behind the grille could not possibly blame you. You were deceived by poor wicked me, and it was all for love. But see, these things are for you.' He held the parcel towards her. She came forward a pace. He put the parcel on the table. 'I had them made specially for you.' He began to unwrap the parcel. 'They are mere toys, I know. But each is a faithful copy of the ornaments carved on the statues of the goddesses at Khajuraho.' He put his head on one side and raised his right hand in a Scout's honour gesture, save that the fingers were curved back like a dancer's. Slowly he took out each ornament – bangles, necklaces, cords of beads for her waist, an elaborate headdress – and held them up before her. 'Do you not hear the sweet tones of the flute, the steady beating of the tabla, the clash of cymbals as they bring you, most adored of the world and heaven, to the palace of the king?' As she began to take the things from him, he whistled quietly, beating time with his fingers on the table. 'Do you not hear the hushed murmur of the adoring crowds as they scatter petals in your path?' Bending, he mimed the scattering of petals. She smiled slightly and bowed. 'You enter the temple and pay homage to the lingam of Siva. Then your handmaidens come to take away your travelling clothes and to adorn you for the king.' He stretched out a hand, and still humming and rocking slightly, placed it on the cross lying at her throat.

'No. He. . . they, will come soon.' She placed her hand over his. Her eyes widened and she caught her breath as his hand, still holding the cross, started to caress her throat.

'Not yet. There is time. Did you not know that India was the larva of the most beautiful butterfly ever to wing her away between heaven and earth?' He caressed and held the flesh of her plump shoulder. 'But the Western wasp came and stung the gorgeous larva as it lay sleeping on a couch of petals, and paralysed her so that she remained as living food for the wasp's children or for any passing predator. And you, my darling child, more than all others, are that gorgeous larva, the latent butterfly of the gods. And I, who know the secrets, am the only one who can remove the poison of that sting and set you free.' He bent and sucked gently at the flesh of her shoulder. 'Hush. Do not tremble. They will not come. I deceived you for love. But first your handmaiden must undress you and prepare you to meet the king.' He removed the cross.

When she was naked and adorned, he too stripped and they stood together naked before the dressing table mirror.

'Now, you and I have no need of these,' said Arun Sen removing the bottles of drink from the dressing table and putting them on the floor. Proudly they stood together before the stained mirror of that cheap piece of warped furniture, his hand supporting her breast, and with the other hand he tapped the rhythm of a song of joy, humming it and occasionally singing the words. She started to join in the singing. As they turned to each other and embraced, they forgot the dingy room and their former fear of being discovered. Their voices rose together without fear as their limbs entwined, and for a moment they became prince and princess, god and goddess.

On the road not far away, the principal and Banglaratnam out for an evening stroll, paused to listen with pleasure to the song. The school problems they had been discussing were carried away by the song. Refreshed, they continued on their way to the ruined fortress.

Miss Willcox and Arun Sen lay together on the couch, she staring at the ceiling, he now turning again the pages of his book and laughing occasionally.

'Look at this one, Sheila. His woman is supported by two others as she mounts the standing king. Now that would be something. Do you think you could find two others to help us in our love? The nurse, of course, would be easy, but she has not good breasts.'

Miss Willcox raised herself quickly and looked at him with hatred. 'You have had her, I knew it.'

'Who says so? But what if I have. It is not important. Everybody has. But if you do not like the idea, forget it. There are always servant girls. One I notice is very ripe, but not yet even betrothed. If Macgregor had servant girls to wait on him, why should not we?'

'Untouchables? You are despicable!' She tugged at the ornaments, ripping them off. 'You practically rape me, now I am to take part in your orgies with untouchables.' She pulled on her clothes.

He still lay naked on the couch, watching her with amusement. 'But yours would be the major part. I simply want handmaidens for you.' He went to her and tried to embrace her. She pushed him away. Angrily he grabbed her by the nape of the neck and

66

forced her over to the mirror. 'Look at yourself, Christian. Look at the colour of your face compared to mine.' He released her and gave her a push towards the door. 'Now get out, and go and do penance tomorrow morning with your other untouchable friends. I too must cleanse myself.'

The principal and Banglaratnam, returning from their walk, were surprised by the sight of a dishevelled Miss Willcox running breathless up to the road.

'Who is that?' shouted the principal. 'No. Stop running away. Come over here.' Miss Willcox came slowly up to them, trying to tidy her hair. 'Miss Willcox, what are you doing out alone so late? Why are you in such a condition?'

'It was such a beautiful evening, sir, that I decided to go for a walk.' She tried to catch her breath and fumbled with her blouse. 'But I came across an enormous python, sir. It frightened me to death! May I go, sir, it has been such a shock. I will never go out alone at night again.'

'Yes, yes. Go!' She ran off. 'These women, Banglaratnam! There is no trusting them.'

'Totally no trusting them.'

'What was I saying? Ah yes. At all costs we must not lose Mr Priestman. You realize, Banglaratnam, that by Western standards his salary is very modest. But we cannot afford more. So to make up for it, we must entertain him. He must never become bored. And above all, he must be kept away from such women as that. They would unsettle him dreadfully. There would be rumours to distress him.'

'The nurse, of course, understands Englishmen.'

'Banglaratnam, Edward Priestman is not Macgregor. Mr Priestman is the very best sort of Englishman. His family have such a long and distinguished connection with India.'

'Such distinguished connections.'

'True. So thank goodness he will be visiting the Maharani. There he will meet nice ladies of his own type. He will correspond with their friendly brothers, and visit them all in the summer holidays to play tennis. How jolly it will be for him!'

'He may come to the south.'

'Yes, yes. Come, we must not roam too far. Is there such a snake?'

'There is very probaby such a snake.'
'A python, the woman said. That is non-poisonous, isn't it?'
'Yes, it is very non-poisonous.'

10

Saturday afternoon Priestman had not felt well enough to call on the Rajah, and postponed his visit till the following week.

On Sunday morning, two buses left the fort for the village of Bhonsa. The bus containing Priestman, Panwar and Banglaratnam departed only after some difficulty. The driver, failing to obtain ignition, climbed out, picked up a large rock, and struck the battery with it. That did the trick. Everybody laughed.

It was in a happy mood, therefore, that the journey began, and Priestman remarked with interest and wonder the many sights to be seen through the window: clusters of huts, a river, a brightly coloured bird which flew in front of the bus and darted away to the right. But as the journey progressed, other members of the staff present stared with increasing gloom through the windows. Nothing they saw seemed to give them pleasure. Priestman questioned Panwar on many subjects, but the answers he received were so vague that he soon gave it up. 'Are these people all strangers in their own country?' thought Priestman. 'They don't know the names of birds or trees, they know nothing of agriculture, and very little about the people. That nearly naked man covered in ash and paint, is "some sort of holy man"; that bullock cart driver with shaven head save for a short pigtail is "some sort of farmer".'

'He is probably a dacoit by night,' added Panwar. 'They are a very dangerous people. They are all dacoits by night.'

Now the village. Welcomes, garlands, sweet little girls in white dresses and scarves. Nervous village onlookers. The woman marshalling the children before songs; her low, sweeping gestures as she turns to face the audience, as though she were ready to fall at somebody's knees. The village elders upright and seemingly fierce, their heads held back in nervousness. And there, right at the back and grinning at Priestman, was Ram Swarup at whom Priestman smiled. Ram Swarup put his hands together, and bowed so low that he disappeared from sight.

The visitors played their part, which consisted mainly of strained smiles, alternated swiftly with airs of extreme weariness. Priestman reflected that they had, perhaps, been practising these expressions as the bus drew closer to the village, and that that was the reason for their increasing solemnity. The visitors' movements grew more languid. They examined the seats provided for them with suspicion before finally, and apparently reluctantly, condescending to sit.

Embarrassed speech by, presumably, the headman. The microphone is faulty. A young man in shorts rushes up to adjust it when it emits metallic honks and ear-splitting howls. Priestman, sitting on the principal's right, noted that the proper way to listen to such a speech was to examine one's shoes, look up at the sky, adjust one's clothes, and address the occasional remark to one's neighbour.

Then the principal came wearily to the microphone, touched it, whereupon it complained dismally, and turned to Priestman to apologize that his speech must be in Hindi, but that he would keep it short. Several times Priestman heard his name mentioned during the speech, and he nodded and smiled up at the principal. 'I am an asset,' thought Priestman. 'But I am also a fraud. My work, such as it is, has nothing to do with all this honour showered upon me. I am not really a teacher. It is simply a convenient way of revisiting the country, trying to stir up old memories. I am simply passing through. These people do not affect me. They sit beside and before me in their colourful, interesting costumes like characters on a processional float. And they are fixed. The middle-aged teachers have no escape save once a year in summer to a small upstairs flat in some unfashionable hill resort. The younger men are becoming like them. But I am just visiting. I am capable of extension. My education, nationality and energy make anything possible for me. And since I am one of the favoured and advantaged of this world, it is my duty to pay back the world with work and initiative; to help put things right. Eventually I must decide how and where I shall crystallize all the past and all my present experiences and those to come. But it is not here, not now, not yet that that decision need be made. And what would I really like to do now? First I would get up, descend this platform and go and sit cross-legged among those snotty-nosed little children, who eye me with such wonder, for I feel closer to them than to anybody else here.'

After the speeches, there was entertainment: village wrestling; a cycle race in which Karatpore school boys competed with Bhonsa village boys who, though several years older, could scarcely keep their balance; some tame rodeo stuff with long-suffering bullocks. Finally, there was a short football match between school and villagers, the village boys lashing out with bare feet at the ball, and falling hard on the rocky ground. Then it was time for lunch. The cautious visitors had brought their own food which was served by their own servants.

After lunch, Priestman wandered around the village with Panwar while the other members of the staff sat in the shade, and the principal went off to discuss some village affairs. As Panwar watched Priestman, he considered their relationship: 'With him I am made secure. Alone, I am such a pitiable creature. I lie on my bed wondering whether it will be safe for me to get up, cross the room and make coffee; what will happen to me, I wonder, during all those movements necessary to perform those simple actions? Will I experience anguish and disappointment? Edward, now, does not consider his every move in advance. He does not know even that he is making such moves. Look at him now; he is too busy thinking of other things as he wanders round the village, biting his lower lip, asking questions, laughing out loud. Does he know all my weaknesses? No, but he senses my general weakness, my constant worry over my health. When I said that November could be treacherous for the health, and that perhaps he should wear a hat, he frowned and shook his head as though a fly had settled on it. When I said that we could not bathe in that river we passed for who knows if there may not be crocodiles, and there are many dangerous germs, he simply snorted. He is brave but foolish, and how much I admire him! But he will always be a stranger in this country. He will never understand.

71

He does not want to. If he did, he would no longer be an Englishman. He is free. I am not free even to cross this path, let alone go to the other side of the world and teach.'

Attracted by the sound of laughter, Priestman and Panwar followed a lane till they came to the outskirts of the village. There on some open ground beside a stream, they found women washing clothes. The women laughed together. Then they would pause to twist a garment till it resembled a thong, and vigorously slap it down on the flat stones. *Slap, Slap!* went the garments raising spray which hung in the air dazzling and causing little rainbows. There was the smell of strong soap, the thick smell of starch – all strong like the sinews in the arms of the women, like their bare backs, and like the stones and their laughter. And all this was so near to the tension in the village, yet utterly apart from it, as though they were all somewhere else far away.

Panwar and Priestman returned slowly into the village, and Panwar thought: 'I must work hard to keep our friendship on an equal footing. Already I can sense that he is slipping away from me. Our intimacy of the first few days is being replaced by his tendency to command me. He is a born and a trained leader; it is so much more natural for him to command than to talk gently of things. Already I am scared to open a conversation with him. He has simply used me to get his bearings. Soon he will wave me goodbye when he finds that I am inadequate and can tell him nothing more. See, he is asking that man questions about metal pans, about plates and pots. Language is no barrier to his friendly interest. Already he knows that I will not have the answer. What do I know about these people's lives? What do I care? A pot is a pot. It is used for something, then thrown away when no longer fit for use. So I am a pot.'

Panwar's sense of humour got the better of his gloom, and he laughed. Priestman heard him.

'So what's the joke? Let me in on it?'

'I was thinking some people are like pots. I am a pot.'

'Rubbish. Though I can see you have the makings of one, and that if you lie on your bed all day, you may very well become one. Exercise is the thing! Ask this man if there is any jungle round here, and we will go and explore it.'

Panwar asked the man, his face and voice becoming severe as

72

he spoke to the lower caste. Priestman frowned at the lack of civility, considering with irritation how everybody was either above or below somebody else in India, and that it was a very tiresome state of affairs from which he was free. Life, he considered, was a battle to avoid taking seriously what others took seriously, and to find out what was really worth taking seriously oneself. 'I do not know yet what that thing is, but I shall find out eventually.'

The villager was gesturing vaguely to the left in order to indicate the location of the jungle.

'Where is it?' asked Priestman. 'What does he say?'

'Over there.'

'How far?'

'Not far. There is a path.'

'So let's go. No, on second thoughts, I shall go alone.'

As Priestman set off up the path leading away from the village, the sky was hazy with heat and dust. His attempt to dress respectably for the event in a tweed suit, though wearing no vest and thin socks, now made his progress uphill uncomfortably hot. He paused and moved round to the shaded side of a large rock. But out of the sun, the wind which now blew steadily from the north, made him shiver. Never before had he experienced such a contrast in temperature. It was necessary to move on.

A hundred yards from the village and half way up the hill, Priestman encountered a blind man crouching behind a makeshift lean-to in a hollow near the path. The man stood up, and turned in Priestman's direction. Priestman stopped to watch the man whose head now turned from side to side as though scenting the wind. Banglaratnam came up behind Priestman and startled him. He led Priestman to one side.

'You are going exploring all by yourself? Marvellous!'

Priestman looked at the country, at the long line of hills so uniform and flattened at the top, at the small patches of thorn trees.

'Yes, I think I'll just take a brisk walk over this hill and see what's on the other side. I need some exercise after my days of forced confinement.'

'Ah, you English. Always the explorers, such energy. We leave in three quarters of an hour precisely. I wish you would take the boys with you. It would be so good for them to walk with you. Besides, you may stumble, and this weather is very treacherous. You should wear a hat.'

'How kind you are. I shall be perfectly alright. Besides, I shan't be away more than twenty minutes or so.'

Banglaratnam moved off down the slope. The blind man hobbled closer.

'English sahib will give five rupees.' His voice was imperious and strangely high-pitched. He was tall, thin and upright. His hair was long and matted. He was far from clean.

'English sahib will give nothing,' said Priestman.

'What! Not give?'

'Not one anna.'

'Why not give?' The beggar cocked his head on one side and smiled.

'Because I won't be ordered about by anyone. And I certainly won't be ordered to give somebody anything.'

'English sahib is rich. Three rupees,' said the man decisively as though they had concluded a bargain.

'I don't bargain. I've told you. Nothing.' Priestman moved off briskly.

'You will give!' shouted the beggar.

Priestman rounded on him.

'Shut up!'

Down the hill, Priestman could make out the figure of Banglaratnam who seemed to be shouting something to him, but the wind carried his words away. Then Banglaratnam waved his hand from side to side. Priestman waved cheerily, and turned to continue his climb.

The blind man began to curse him long and hard in a falsetto scream. Priestman quickened his stride to get away from the irritating stream of noise. Sweat trickled down his face, and the hardness of the earth in some places, and the way in which it crumbled easily in others, caused him to stumble. He soon became out of breath, but was anxious to top the rise and escape from the sound of the man whose piercing tones the force of the wind did not diminish.

He paused for breath at the top, and looked down at the blind man and at the village beyond. It seemed strange to him that

74

there was no longer any sign of activity in the village. And it occurred to him that all he had to do was to walk away from that place, and to keep walking, and that all the things that had happened to him during the past week, and the people he had met would cease to exist. The beggar's face still pointed in his direction, but the lips now moved silently as though his mouth too had lost its faculties. It seemed obvious to Priestman that this was not the man he had been told about by one of the boys. Ashok, was it? No. That man was a holy man, a healer of many ills, curer of snake bite. Not a filthy, importunate beggar.

'You poor, bloody fool,' muttered Priestman in the direction of the beggar. 'If only you had asked politely, I would have probably given you something.'

He turned away from the village, and saw to his left in the middle distance a valley a mile or so wide between two flat-topped hills. Along the middle of the valley walked a camel led by its driver. They seemed the only living things in that waste. And it came to him suddenly that India as he had visualized it, as a map with political boundaries, was not like that at all; that the political boundaries were of no real significance, that this land stretched on and on through jungles, ruins, deserts, mountains and ice, and that it always had done so, no matter what people did to it. He felt the expanse of the world, something that he had not experienced in cultivated, signposted little England.

The camel stopped and sat down heaving and grumbling. The noise came to him clearly, like a series of deliberate belches, for some reason strangely satisfying to Priestman. The driver mounted, and turned the camel away from its earlier direction. They made off fast towards the north. The camel's legs moving in the haze looked as though they were passing easily through water. Then animal and rider disappeared suddenly, presumably into a ravine on the other side of the valley which Priestman had not seen. But why they should suddenly change direction seemed to him a mystery that he would never solve.

Once again, the combination of fierce sun and chilling wind forced Priestman to move on. Besides, there was nothing interesting to see; only another flat-topped hill like the one he was on. He descended the slope. It was hard to keep his balance. The path had either petered out, or he had lost it in his haste to get away. There seemed no feature that he could make for, and already it seemed as though the little village, its inhabitants and his friends had ceased to exist altogether simply because of the separation by one hilltop.

The bottom of the *nullah*, or dried watercourse, between the hills was cracked. He climbed the next hill, and found a similar *nullah* with steeper sides, and the opposite side was too steep to climb. He followed the *nullah* in the hope that it would lead somewhere interesting, or that the opposite bank would become easier to climb. The light grey colour of the earth reflected the sun painfully into his eyes. He began to wonder what he expected to find that would qualify as interesting: animals, people, vegetation, buildings, water?

Now there were frequent bends in the *nullah*. He wondered whether he wanted to meet a tiger, but decided with a smile that he did not, unless it proved friendly.

On turning the next bend, he came upon two naked little girls bathing a buffalo in a muddy pool. The water reached half way up the buffalo's flanks. One girl, who seemed about seven or eight, moved round in the water to the other side of the animal to hide her nakedness. The smaller girl, about five or six years old, clambered on to the animal's back, and lay down, pressing her belly against the hard ridge of its spine. She slapped the beast's flank, kicked it with her heels, and said, '*aré*' softly. The buffalo twisted round its supple neck, shot out its tongue at her, then moved forward a pace.

'Hello there!' called Priestman, smiling broadly.

The girls watched him attentively but without fear, as deer in a park watch a human who approaches too near. Priestman stood still, wondering what they would do. And they did the same. There was the cut-grass smell of warm dung and the faintly oily aroma of disturbed mud.

Then a man appeared as if from nowhere, and eyeing Priestman all the time, spoke to the girls, who replied briefly. The smaller girl kicked the buffalo again, while the older one moved round in the water to its near side.

Priestman smiled at the man, and waved a cheery greeting. He asked by signs if the animal and girls were his. The man nodded, and moving away from the pool, beckoned Priestman to follow

76

him. Priestman consulted his watch, and was surprised to note that only five or ten minutes had elapsed since leaving the vice-principal. He decided to follow the man.

Priestman looked back at the girls. They were still in the same position, still watching him. He thought it sad that they were so prudish so young. He would have liked to see them splashing unashamedly, to have taken pleasure in the freedom of their nakedness. 'I, too,' he thought, 'would like to bathe naked with them; to be unafraid of a fat old buffalo; to slap his slatey flank, and cry '*aré*'. Instead, I shall go to this man's village, and be shown how neat and clean it all is, how brightly burnished are their little pots. And I shall give them the money that I would have given the beggar had he been polite. Well, at least it will be my own find. I shall find my own Indian village. It will not be a showpiece, but the real thing.'

As they climbed upwards, the wind became stronger sending grit into their eyes. Priestman kept his head down and fixed his eyes on the bare heels of his guide, heels so cracked that they seemed to Priestman miniature versions of the landscape they were passing through. 'So this is the jungle. I must adjust my ideas to the fact that India is mainly a desert, not a tropical rain forest.'

So fierce was the wind, and irritating the dust, that Priestman did not realize he was in a village until he saw, out of the corner of one eye, a mud wall whose base was pitted and crumbling. He stopped and raising his head, looked around. There seemed to be just one narrow lane on to which gave small doors raised on platforms. He thought for a moment that he heard the sound of running water, then realized that it was the sound of hundreds of rats rustling the thatch of the buildings. Chaff or the stalks of some crop blew down the lane and caught in his hair. His guide had disappeared. The place seemed deserted.

Then one by one, small children mostly naked save for the older girls who were in rags, came forward out of the haze and gathered silently round him. Their limbs were hideously thin, the bodies of many were covered with sores, and flies gathered undisturbed on their eyes. Then the circle of children gave way before him to admit the sight of others who, too weak to walk, dragged themselves through the dust towards him.

77

11

At Bhonsa, the visitors were anxious to be off. Panwar thought that if it were not for this ridiculous notion of punctuality which stated they must leave in quarter of an hour, they would have left long ago. The villagers did not know whether to get on with their lives, or whether to keep themselves in readiness for any request from their guests. The boys lounged about, bored. Groups of masters talked spasmodically. And to Panwar it seemed that they and he were boring while Edward, roaming around on his own, was laying down new impressions, storing them up for some future day when he would amuse his friends, impress colleagues in some more important job by saying, 'No, India is not like that, it is like this. We should do this and that about India.' And now here was Banglaratnam, that essentially kind but silly man, coming to pester him with questions.

'Well, Panwar, our Englishman is running true to form again, tramping over the countryside. I tell you there is no stopping them. He is such an asset to the school.'

'I hope he will be back on time,' said Panwar irritated that he had not been praised as an asset, and that Priestman had not invited him along.

'Of course he will be back on time. They are all very punctual.'

'That is true. But this country is so very wild, so broken up and featureless. He may miss his way. It is his first walk alone in India, he told me. From dacoits and other malicious persons he has little to fear, I suppose, until sunset. Snakes of course abound. But still he is strong and fearless. They all are. He would not care to notice such things.'

'I was not told of this,' said Banglaratnam becoming agitated.

78

'His first walk, you say. You should have told me. We could have prevented him. Only five minutes before the bus leaves, and still he is not back.'

Priestman came running down the hill.

'Ha! There he is, bang on time as I told you!' cried Banglaratnam. 'Hello there! Do not run. You have plenty of time. Yes, the blind beggar has gone, you are safe to pass.'

'You must come immediately,' panted Priestman joining them and taking Banglaratnam by the arm. 'There is a village over there. People are starving. Sick. They are dying at this moment. Little children. We must do something to help now.'

'Starving, you say?' queried Banglaratnam. 'How is that possible? There is no report of famine. No, no. These people, I tell you, can be very cunning. They will make you believe such things just to get money.'

'Well I have seen it. This is no put-up job. We must tell the principal. Ask for help.'

'By all means. We must certainly inform the principal.'

'You are sweating and shivering, Edward,' said Panwar.

'Yes, dear boy,' said Banglaratnam. 'Are you sure you have not caught some fever? You are up too soon after your illness.'

'I agree that I've been hurrying and am shivering. But that is one thing. What I have seen is another, and demands immediate action.'

They walked down to the principal, Priestman hurrying ahead. The principal acted with great concern at the news. He called the headman of the village, and spoke to him in Hindi.

'This man says there is no village in that direction. The nearest village in any direction is five miles away down that track.' The principal turned again and spoke with the headman. 'He says it is a big village, bigger than this, and that it is richer than Bhonsa. The people there are certainly not starving.'

'Well, could I have reached the outskirts of that village, or some suburb of it, or some hamlet near it?'

'No, no,' interjected Banglaratnam. 'That is out of the question. You could not have gone more than one mile.'

The other members of staff had gathered round.

'More like five furlongs,' said the mathematics teacher, Mattacharya.

79

'Five or six furlongs at most,' agreed the geography master, Patel.

'Perhaps,' said Panwar diffidently, 'it was a wandering group of people you met. Gypsies or some such.'

'No. They had huts solidly built and thatched. There was a narrow main street. But, for heaven's sake, why are we standing around here talking? We must go and help.'

The engines of the two buses started up. Servants climbed aboard to make sure that the seats were clean for their masters. Others made sure that all the lunch things and other baggage, such as the art master's easel, were securely stowed.

'We can't just leave,' said Priestman.

Some of the boys who had overheard the conversation, were excited and suggested that Priestman should lead them to the place.

'No, no. That is out of the question,' said Banglaratnam. 'You would miss your tea.'

'What we shall do,' said the principal with decision, 'is to go back to school now. There, I shall immediately telephone the block medical office and the police. They know all the people in this area. They will understand the problem, and be in a good position to take immediate and effective action. I assure you, Edward, that is the best plan. We are unfortunately not equipped to help.'

'That's a good idea,' said Priestman, 'but couldn't we call in on them on the way?'

'That could cause delay. They may not be in at this time on a Sunday. Come, let us go.'

They went towards the buses.

'But why does that headman or whatever he is say there is no village there?' asked Priestman.

'These people,' said Banglaratnam. 'They do not know everything. Why, even things happening a few miles from them, they know nothing about. It is a very backward part.'

'Perhaps he is afraid to lose some of your patronage to those poor people. They may even be outcastes from his own village.'

The principal nodded, and everyone boarded the bus quickly, as though anxious to get away from the place and the event, whatever it had been, that had caused so much questioning and uncertainty. A lie, madness, or tragedy was in the air. It was somebody's fault. A guest had been exposed to an unseemly aspect of India, and there had been no one with him to explain it.

To Priestman, the reactions of the staff seemed inexplicable. It would have taken them only fifteen minutes or so simply to go and see. They could have taken the worst cases in the buses to hospital, brought food to the others from Bhonsa.

In the bus, Priestman confided to Panwar that there was no doubt in his mind that the headman was lying, and that there was something underhand about the man, and that his replies to the principal had been evasive. Panwar agreed, but was worried for his friend, and asked again if he were feeling well.

'Oh, good God,' said Priestman trying to control himself. 'Why all this constant harping on one's health? Children, old people are dying out there, and you go on about my fever. And please remember that in English "fever" means something serious like "yellow fever", not just a slight temperature, which seems to be your meaning.'

After this outburst, Priestman remained silent and tight-lipped for the rest of the journey, only managing a smile when the principal and vice-principal turned round to ask how he was feeling. The vice-principal came and sat near Priestman, and began a discourse on the excellence of the last monsoon and harvest, and the extreme unlikelihood of any local famine.

'How strange,' said Priestman trying to remain polite. 'But the place exists, the people are diseased and starving. One does not have to be an expert in these things to see that. Anyway, the matter will soon be cleared up, and help on its way.'

They drove into the school.

In the village of Bhonsa, Ram Swarup and his helpers Choti Lal and Bhagat Chand had shown the photographs of Amanti. Now they sat eyeing the prospective son-in-law and his father. Ram Swarup had felt that the negotiations were going well. Priestman's photography had created a good impression. Priestman himself had cut a fine figure for him, strolling around the village, smiling and chatting to its inhabitants. His behaviour after his walk, however, had created unexpected difficulties.

'It is said,' opened Ram Swarup, 'that my master will in all probability become the new principal.'

'Ha,' said the other man, and indicated a bowl of sweets. Ram Swarup smiled, refused, was pressed again to take one, refused again and took one. 'My family has served the headman's family for ten generations.'

Ram Swarup was about to say, 'that is as it should be'. But he became suspicious that his father was being blamed for selling a similar birthright in order to go off and serve the English during the time of the Raj, thereby gaining good money but eventually losing status. How was his father to know that the Empire would come to an end? It was all the doing of his wife's family, and particularly of that utterly travelled man, her father.

'Ha,' he said without commitment. There was a polite pause during which more delicacies were offered.

'I understand that the English have strong opinions about various matters,' said the other man, referring obliquely to Priestman's vehement behaviour after his walk.

'They are indignant in the face of poverty,' said Ram Swarup. 'Their hearts are moved to pity.'

'And their purses?' queried the prospective father-in-law, considering that if this new Englishman were to become principal, he might well increase the school's grant to the village.

'Moved to pity also,' said Ram Swarup. His colleagues, Choti Lal and Bhagat Chand, nodded agreement.

'Education is a wonderful thing,' said the villager. The others all nodded agreement. Ram Swarup now considered that the crisis had passed, and that his connection with the school was being given its due. 'The American missionaries who were here two years ago were so pleased with my son's progress.' The man turned to his son who said:

'It's a fine day, Belle Memsahib. I'm a very good boy.'

For a moment, Ram Swarup was nonplussed. He had to think fast. 'That is good, excellent. My daughter too is taking English lessons.'

'Good, good. Show the certificate.'

A box was brought, and from it extracted a paper on which was written: 'This is to certify that Bhang Pradeep is a thoro' trustworthy servant, who has made good progress in English.

Signed Belle Midlestraum.'

'My daughter will soon receive her first certificate when she has completed her primary course with my master,' concluded Ram Swarup wondering how he could possibly get such a paper.

12

On the Tuesday after the visit to Bhonsa, Priestman was informed by the principal that after a thorough search by the authorities, the starving village could not be found. That evening, Priestman sat disconsolate and angry in the principal's bungalow with the principal and a visitor to the school.

'Mr Agrawal has been so looking forward to meeting you, Edward,' said the principal.

Priestman nodded and smiled at the visitor. He was a neat old man who, Priestman imagined, must always look as he did now – freshly powdered from his bath and calmly ready for the world. The visitor cocked his head. His eyes were inquisitive and playful as he watched Priestman. Priestman considered what a pleasure it was for an Englishman always to be made so welcome in India. If there was hate or at least resentment in this man, who had been imprisoned, it was said, by the British in his fiery disobedient youth, how far must that hate now be buried. Or rather, it was as though he had absorbed it or placed it on a level where it no longer touched him.

'Mr Agrawal is very knowledgeable about the British,' continued the principal, laughing away at his own joke. 'He was so frequently the guest of his majesty, the king emperor.'

Agrawal began to relate stories of his imprisonment. He had splendid relations with his captors, all save one police officer, a stickler for discipline and a figure of fun to his colleagues and captors alike. Then there was the young British officer who went out of his way to get extra books for Agrawal, made sure that he had plenty of writing materials.

'I was so afraid,' he said, his eyes amazed and childlike. 'I was sure they would torture me that first day when I was taken into custody. Into my cell comes a young police officer. This is it, I thought. Instead, he says gently, "I am afraid you may not be very comfortable here, Mr Agrawal." Mr he calls me! I was flabbergasted. "Do you require anything?" he asks me. "Please do not hesitate to tell me if I can bring you anything." '

And now, that one young man's consideration seemed to have continued through the years till it became a kind of love welling in the room where they sat, so that Priestman felt close to tears and simply shook his head. Agrawal reached forward and lightly touched his arm. They were so instantly friends.

Then the principal told Priestman how Agrawal had worked for years improving the lot of the poor throughout India. Names of organizations and the various movements with which he was connected or had founded were mentioned. Then Agrawal spoke of his English friends, Americans, Canadians, Australians, New Zealanders and many others who were all helping with this work; their prayers, their selfless gifts. Priestman was lost in this network of common endeavour which seemed to span the globe, but of which he had only vaguely heard before. And it was apparent that this one, small man before him, so famous and so revered, was the inspiration for all this activity. And yet he was giving Priestman his greatest attention, asking his opinion and listening with the utmost care to Priestman's replies.

'I hear that you, too, are interested in village work, Mr Priestman; I do so wish you would help us. If only you were not doing such a marvellous job here! But perhaps your principal will lend you to us. You could be of so much help, and we are in such need.'

'No, no!' said the principal. 'I will never let you have Edward. You will not succeed in taking him away from us. You must not listen to him, Edward, or he will have you squatting in some village hut being his schoolmaster. The untouchables will all be speaking Oxford English.'

The little man did not laugh, but watched Priestman attentively.

'I gather, however, that you have already had some experience of how bad village conditions can be,' said Agrawal.

'A most horrifying experience,' chimed in the principal. 'A band of wandering, poor people, tribals no doubt. Poor Edward

85

came across them where they had taken shelter in some abandoned ruin or other. And Edward's first trip alone into the countryside. He was quite convinced that they were starving. He is not used to seeing the very poor. So violent and sudden a contrast with England. And it is most distressing. A very thorough search has been made by the authorities, but nobody can find them or the village.'

'Please tell me about the village, Mr Priestman,' said Agrawal.

'Yes, Edward will do that. But you must really both excuse me, I have a very urgent meeting with housemasters. Please forgive me, and ask for anything you want. Oh, and you haven't forgotten, Edward, that you are calling on the Rajah tomorrow. Yes? Good.' The principal spoke to the two servants in the room, and departed.

'Tell me. This village?' asked Agrawal, once they were alone.

'I begin to doubt its existence myself.' He described the village and its people, Agrawal nodding from time to time. 'But the strange thing is that the buildings were well constructed, or had been at one time, and were thatched.'

'That is interesting. A thatched village in this area is most unusual. They do not use it here. Tell me about the house construction, if you can. Though you were there so short a time that it must be difficult to have taken in any details.'

'Not at all. It is all extremely clear to me. There was a raised platform in front of many of the houses. It came up to the region of my chest. Some of these platforms were of stone, and others of baked mud. Wooden posts embedded in the platform supported the roof.'

'And the people. What did they look like?'

'Well, as I said I saw only children at first. But then the adults came. They seemed smaller and darker than the villagers round here. And the men don't wear shirts. Anyway their dark colour made me think they were probably nomadic; I suppose because Europeans think of gypsies as dark.'

'No, I do not think they were nomads. I do not for a moment doubt the existence of the village and of its inhabitants. No, not for a moment.' When he said this, his manner was very serious and firm. Then his demeanour changed, and gave way to a glowing smile which seemed to emanate from an inner peace and conviction, as though he had known all along what the answer had been about this strange village of Priestman's, and that Priestman's answers had simply confirmed his opinion.

'I can't tell you how glad I am to hear you say that. I was beginning to think I had gone crazy.'

'Certainly not. The village exists, though it may not be quite where you think it is.'

'I agree. I once felt certain of its location. Now I'm not so sure. The country is so broken up and similar in features. And there was such a duststorm at the time. Still, I can't for the life of me understand how the authorities have been unable to find it. It must be within a mile or so from Bhonsa. It must have been a very perfunctory search. Of course, another possibility is that they did in fact find the place, and for some reason – shame of exposure to a higher authority, or something even more sinister – are unwilling to say that they've found it. I don't know. It's all very unsatisfactory. And another thing; I feel I've been a nuisance to the principal. After all it isn't his pigeon. You see everything started so well. Everything was so amusing and interesting and colourful. Now it's all gone wrong. I feel angry and dissatisfied with the action, or lack of it, taken up till now. I want to kick up a row. Be in charge of a proper search. Sort it out. But that would be offensive to my hosts, and . . . anyway, you can see that I don't know what to do. It's all very perplexing.'

'India can be very perplexing to a visitor. It can play many tricks. Of course, we do not think of them as tricks. We accept phenomena which may not have a rational explanation. I see you frown. Let me put it this way; most Indians would not think it strange if they could not find the village again. They would put its disappearance, and its appearance, down to something else. Now I see I have offended you. You think that I, too, am suggesting that your mind was affected in some way. Well, what if it was? That does not make you mad. If a man is intoxicated by liquor or drugs, or is under the control of a hypnotist, neither you nor I would necessarily call him crazy, though he may see and do things not in his everyday experience and character. Drugs and drink we can discount. . .'

'Mr Agrawal, please don't think me so naive as to discount all those possibilities out of hand. However, I discount them in my

87

case. An Indian may well be susceptible to hallucinations, just as a Roman Catholic peasant may want to have a vision of the Virgin Mary and so goes ahead and has one. If I wanted to have a vision of India, I should choose to make it one of the tropical lagoon palm-fronted variety complete with suitable female props. No, I am not at all angry. I am just a practical man unafraid of my subconscious, unimpressed by my collective unconscious, and the two brushes I have had with the paranormal – one in England, the other in Spain – I found irritating and boring. And as to Hamlet's father's ghost or Banquo's ghost or any other manifestations indicating guilt because of things done or left undone, well I have no such feelings. And anyway, are you really so sure you have the answer with all your good works and your international prayers? I'm sorry; that was unjust. Forgive me. But you see, I can't help thinking of those poor people, of the children, their faces. They were looking to me for help. I was their only chance, their last chance. I spoke to them. I know their names. I was to come back with help. But I have failed them. This is hopeless. I thought you at least would understand.'

'I do understand. Try not to be so unhappy about it all. These things happen all the time. Generally, there is sufficiency of grain. But so many villagers are very isolated. We cannot be everywhere, though we should like to be. But you say you know their names. That is very interesting. Can you tell me their names, describe individuals? It will all be of help.'

'Of course I will. But how will it help?'

'I do have many friends and sources of information.'

So Priestman described several of the children and gave Agrawal their names, and Agrawal noted it all down in a little book whose blue cardboard cover bore the legend 'Jumble Paddings'. Priestman could not help uttering a brief laugh when he saw it, and to Agrawal's enquiring smile, he explained: 'Oh, it was just the title of your notebook. It seems as though somebody started to make an anagram, then got muddled and gave up.'

'You like doing crosswords?'

'I used to do *The Times* crossword most days, but I wouldn't here. Just like Herr Bach. No. It's nothing. What were you saying?'

'I was going to ask how you get on with your servant. Ram Swarup and his wife are old friends of mine. Their daughter is a lovely child. So alert and full of understanding. Sometimes I think I would love to take her with me on my travels. But all the servants are such friends of mine.' Priestman looked gloomy and distracted, so Agrawal continued. 'I suppose you must have read many books about India, and seen films and television documentaries too? The principal tells me your family has such a long connection with India. It must have been talked about often in your home.'

'I see what you're driving at. That I've simply concocted all this from what I've read or heard. I just find it strange that you seem to have made up your mind that I am the victim of some hallucination, whereas I would put that possibility at a thousand to one.'

'You're wrong that I have made up my mind. And forgive me for saying that if I were to use the word "hallucination", then I would definitely not say that you are a victim of it. I would say rather that you have been blessed with a vision because you are close to God.'

'Oh, really, please!' cried Priestman jumping up. Making towards the door, he added without looking at Agrawal: 'You say that only because you think you are close to God. Goodnight and thank you.' He paused at the door, turned, and walking back swiftly to Agrawal, seized the startled old man's hands in his and looked long into his face. Then, in distress, he hurriedly left the room.

Once outside, he quickly crossed the fifty yards or so to his rooms, vowing as he hurried on that as soon as he could get away for half a day, he would go back and find the village himself. He began to make plans about medical aid and food. He would take the nurse. As he neared the steps to his door, he thought he saw a short figure in the shadows.

'Ashok, if you don't go to bed immediately, I shall have to report you to Mr Patel.' But there was no reply, and when he mounted the steps he found nobody there.

For a while he paced up and down the living room. Then he went into the bedroom, opened a drawer in the dressing table and took out the sheet of proof photographs he had taken of

Amanti. For a long time he studied them under the bedside lamp. Then he put the sheet away beneath the paper lining in the bottom of the drawer.

13

The next morning, after Priestman had left for class, Ram Swarup cleaned out his rooms as usual and noted that Priestman had carelessly stuffed his first month's salary into a drawer of his dressing table. The money amounted roughly to that which Ram Swarup could earn from Priestman during five years.

When he had finished cleaning up, he returned to his room and spoke to his wife. 'I have an idea that has been in my mind. Amanti shall have English lessons from Edward Sahib.'

His wife closed her eyes, and remained silent trying to communicate to him her contempt for the idea and its impropriety. Irritated, he pursued his line of thought. 'You will go and sit with her while she learns. The old sahib would teach anyone for nothing before he became ill. It is their calling. Edward Sahib would do it for less than nothing, and be pleased to do it, I am sure. I know what you are thinking, that a girl of our caste knowing English is improper. But it will raise her value and our prestige in the community. Besides, the Bhonsa boy has a certificate from the American missionaries. . .'

'So you told me. What of it? It occurs to me that these Bhonsa people are too fine for their own good. Besides, he is a boy. Anyway, she will sound cheap. Do you want people to think she is some Anglo-Indian girl? It seems you are all for these Bhonsa people. But before you found them, did you look seriously anywhere else?'

'You know very well that searching for a son-in-law can become a full-time occupation. If I had done that, my work would have suffered, and I would not have been given to Edward Sahib. If I do it now, I will lose him. There are plenty of others ready to take my place. That Garap fellow, now he sees that not

91

all Englishmen kick their servants, would jump at the chance to serve Edward Sahib, particularly since he leaves a thousand rupees stuffed in a drawer for all to take. It is alright. I have locked the place. I will speak to Edward Sahib about the danger of thieves. . .'

'You will be accused of stealing one thousand rupees!'

'Nonsense. He will take it to the bank. I will do it if he will not. I wish I had said nothing of it. But enough of that. Amanti will take English lessons, that is what we are discussing.'

'I thought you had decided and arranged it all. But if you must do this vain thing, why not ask one of the women teachers at the Junior School?'

Ram Swarup wanted to say: 'You gave me only one son and now he is dead. You understand nothing.' Instead he said: 'At least let us do what is best for our daughter and for our community.' His wife supplied the 'only child and a girl' in his reproach.

'You must do what you think best,' she said quietly, and he felt sorry for her.

'She need not have many lessons. After a few, he will give us a signed paper. It will be a precious paper with many seals upon it. She will treasure it all her life, and will pass it on to our grandchildren.'

'You must do what you think best,' she repeated.

'The yogi Agrawal says it is for the best.'

'He is not of our world.'

'Come, it is not as though it would interfere with her work. She has none.'

'We must make a sacrifice at the temple of the goddess. But this morning you must guard his rooms. You should go now and see that nobody has tried to enter.'

On his way back to the dining hall for lunch, Priestman met Miss Willcox for the first time. He smiled and she stopped.

'Mr Priestman, I am so glad to meet you. I hear you had a terrible experience last Sunday.' She was wide-eyed and shook her head from side to side as though the better to grasp any information that might emanate from him. 'But I am so sorry, you must be sick of talking about it.'

She started to move sideways, and Priestman found himself

turning too as though they were a pair of cats. All the time her eyes twinkled as if, in spite of her sympathetic words, she was ready to burst into laughter. Priestman, too, found himself smiling when he realized that for the first time in India he had met a woman with whom he could talk easily.

'I'm afraid,' he said, 'that the episode has been thrown out of focus. It has become a subject for talk, not action. The boys, for example, pester me in class with questions about it as an excuse not to work.'

'How awful. I know. They will seize on any excuse. I am having so much trouble myself with the English play in the Junior School. As a Christian, and English being my first language so to speak, one is saddled with all these things. I'm sure you must be too.'

'What is the play?'

'Oh, a terrible jumped-up sort of thing from "Best Plays for the Kiddies" or some such series. It is really nothing. But if you could possibly come once or twice to rehearsals, it would be so encouraging for the boys, and you could help so much with our terrible pronunciation, and correct my mistakes.'

'Nonsense. Your English is perfect.'

'Oh, you are too kind. You are flattering me, I can see that.' Her eyes continuously moved away from his, watching to see who was observing them. 'But I hear the village you found may not exist?'

'I was told by the principal yesterday that after extensive enquiries by Block Officers, whoever they may be, it does not. But "Block Officers" is not a very reassuring term for investigators, is it?' He laughed and so did she, but it did not seem to Priestman that she had understood the joke.

'So whatever will you do?'

'I shall go there as soon as I can with witnesses. I don't distrust anybody, but I must satisfy myself. Panwar and I plan to cycle out there on Sunday. We shall take some medical supplies. It would, of course, be better if the nurse could come. But I gather she can't, unless chaperoned. I didn't realize how Victorian things are here. For example, this afternoon, I "call" on the Rajah. Anyway, so I haven't asked the nurse.'

'I know, all this old-fashionedness is so irritating. It holds back education so much. But it is all a front you know. Underneath, we can be very modern and free-thinking. Even though I am Catholic, I think I am open to new ideas and suggestions. I suppose I could act as her chaperone if you would have me. But would you want me? I have only done two or three first-aid courses.'

'Well, what a splendid idea. Of course I would love to have you along.'

'Now you are flattering poor me again.'

'Am I? I didn't think so. But one thing; I'm afraid that Arun Sen is not coming. I think I may have offended him, though I can't imagine how. Anyway, he says he's not one for cycle trips.'

'I am not surprised. But why should he come? What has he to do with it? I tell you quite frankly I am glad he is not coming with us. He can be very cynical at times, so people tell me.'

'I see. Now there's my servant hovering about. I wonder what he wants.'

'They are always wanting something, these people. So I shall ask Sunita, the nurse? She will not refuse me.'

'Fine. And I'll get Panwar to let you know about times and other arrangements. So, see you Sunday morning, alright?'

'Yes, excellent. Oh, I must dash! I have lost all track of time talking to you. It is so good to meet somebody intelligent, and somebody who cares about the plight of poor people. Mrs Bhoshi – she was with the poet-saint Tiganji in Nagpur, you know – she is most impressed.'

'Yes? Perhaps I could meet her some time?'

'I would love to introduce you. She is so shy and retiring, but I know I can manage an introduction for you. She is such a famous lady, and so saintly.'

'That's very kind. Just one thing more. I think we should keep the purpose of our trip quiet, don't you?'

'Definitely. The whole trip must be kept quiet. Otherwise some foolish people may be getting the wrong notions.'

Priestman laughed and said goodbye. As he hurried towards the dining hall, Ram Swarup intercepted him. He put his hands together, bowed low, smiled and holding his head to one side, uttered the word 'sahib'. The word lasted for several seconds, and rose and fell through many notes of some strange scale by

94

means of which he hoped to convey deference, anxiety for his master, mild reproach and urgency. But Priestman hurried past him saying: 'Not now, Ram Swarup. I'm late.'

And Ram Swarup bowed once again, hands together, at Priestman's receding back.

After lunch Priestman met Panwar, and they walked together to the classrooms.

'Panwar, why don't you ever eat in hall?'

'School food is not in my contract. I would have to pay.'

'Outrageous! Now about this trip on Sunday. . .' Priestman told him of his arrangements with Miss Willcox. Panwar was full of misgivings, but he was too polite and unsure of himself to utter them with any force.

'Nonsense!' said Priestman. 'Everything will be fine. Anyway, it's all arranged. We definitely need the nurse, and she won't come without the other woman, and she has some training anyway. So you are lumbered with female company for once, old chap. Don't look so miserable. I shall be your chaperone, and defend you stoutly against any assault upon your honour as a superior upper caste Brahmin gentleman, ho, ho! But at least things are moving in the right direction, and we're getting some action at last.'

95

14

On the same day, after school, Priestman walked down to the town to pay his long deferred call on the Rajah. The man at the main entrance to the palace did not seem to understand the purpose of his visit. He pointed to a visitors' book which Priestman dutifully signed.

'Well, what now?' asked Priestman.

'That is alright. Very good,' said the man, nodding in the direction of the signature.

'So you will tell the Rajah that I am here?'

'Not necessary. His Highness will be given the book.'

'When?'

'Sometime. When he asks for it.'

'Kindly tell the Rajah that I am here.'

'Yes, I will tell him,' said the man, and stayed where he was, smiling.

'No. Please go now and tell him that I am waiting!'

'He may not be able to see you.'

'Why not? His Highness is expecting me.'

'Ah. His Highness is expecting you, Mr . . .?'

'Priestman.'

The man went off, and after what seemed a ridiculously long wait to Priestman, returned and ushered him into a large reception hall. After a further wait of five minutes, the Rani came out of a little door from an unexpected direction, and with the long strides so unsuited to such a small woman, came up to him saying: 'I am so sorry. My husband is out. But let us go away from this terrible room. All this marble is so cold in winter, and what you are standing on is not the largest carpet in the world.'

She led him across the object in question, and pointing to the enormous central chandelier, added: 'And that is not the largest chandelier in the world. If they were all the largest in the world, then the terrible taste of the place wouldn't matter so much, would it?'

'No doubt certain tastes have their uses.'

'And this one's use is long past. Come.' She led him into a small comfortable drawing room. Tea and little cakes were brought.

'I'm so glad to find you fully recovered,' said Priestman looking solemn.

The Rani was puzzled for a moment, then laughed. 'Ah, that was my part in the show.'

Priestman smiled, not understanding.

'But I hear you too have not been well,' the Rani prompted.

Priestman related the circumstances of his illness and his colleagues' reaction to it. He elaborated in an amusing vein since it was apparent that she lived a somewhat secluded life, and was eager for news and entertainment. Priestman congratulated himself that in one day he had found two women who apparently liked him and were therefore easy to talk to. They discussed the relative merits of counts Bolkonsky and Rostov.

'And I must tell you the funniest thing,' said the Rani. 'My poor dear mother-in-law believes I will get into trouble with the British for reading seditious Russian novels.'

'Could I not masquerade as a representative of Her Majesty's Government, and reassure her?'

'She would die of fright. She would not see you. She lives in fear of the British. Of course it's very amusing, but it can get a bit irksome, and sometimes I get very impatient about this Russian business.'

'I have an idea. The British Council sent me some information the other day. With a bit of juggling, I could use the heading of their very British writing paper, and send her an official-looking note to the effect that we have looked into the matter, and cleared you of all possible charges of treason.'

'What a splendid idea. It may not do any good. She has such an *idée fixe,* but it would be marvellous to follow her reactions.'

Writing materials were brought, and the following draft letter concocted:

We, the representative of Her Most Imperial Majesty in India, having known for many years of the predilection of Her Highness The Rani of Karatpore for Russian novels, in particular for the work by one Leo Tolstoy entitled *War and Peace*, hereby beg to inform you that, after due consideration, we find nothing remotely seditious or treasonable in these works, and that on the contrary we do hereby approve and heartily recommend them to all our subjects.

We respectfully take this opportunity to remind ourselves of the very great, long-standing and continued loyalty of the House of Karatpore to Her Most Imperial Majesty, and to offer our grateful thanks for the support and kindness always so readily and unstintingly afforded us.

We beg to remain, etc

There was some doubt between the conspirators, for so they now considered themselves, as to how the letter should be signed. They eventually settled for a squiggle above the words 'The Viceroy of India'.

'What a great help you are!' said the Rani. 'I do hope we shall see you often, and that we shall become firm friends.'

'I am very grateful for the support and kindness so unstintingly afforded me,' said Priestman laughing and getting up to leave. The Rani laughed and motioned him back to his chair.

'You're not in a hurry to go? Good. Now there is one further little chore I would ask you to perform for me. You don't mind? Well I gather you are going to spend some time these holidays with the Maharajah of D. . . . and his wife.'

'How news travels, your Highness!'

'Indeed it does. And I have also heard of your unfortunate experience on Sunday. I didn't raise the subject before because I thought it might be distressing to you.'

'I am no longer distressed because I plan soon to conduct some investigations myself. So with action in the offing, I don't feel miserable. Anyway, I'm not the moping type.'

'Well, I may be able to help on that score. I will go into that in a moment. But first, as you said, news travels fast, so I would beg you to be most discreet about what I am going to tell you, and to mention it to no one. No, of course you won't. I forgot that I was talking to an Englishman. So I must tell you that my poor husband is in certain difficulties. Nothing too serious, you understand. But this government is so hard on us; taxes and so on. They will not understand the valuable position we have held for so many centuries in Indian society. I'm not talking about that Durbar hall out there, and all it represented, but of our power in the light of progressive ideas for social change and the good of our subjects. What has happened in this state, Mr Priestman, is that the government has replaced us in name and brought nothing in our place. People will tell you that this was a backward state. But I can tell you it was actually better off before Independence than it is now, and by that I mean that the people, the common people, were better off.'

'That's awful. I know what you mean.'

'Exactly. You have seen for yourself. Incompetence, lack of interest. Now this must be changed, and I think you may be instrumental in bringing about such a change. The Maharajah of D. . ., in contrast to us, is very well in with this government. He has great influence. But, quite frankly, I must tell you that he despises poor Percy. No, it is true. But if the Maharajah were persuaded that there were energetic backing and intelligent, practical ideas for social progress in this state, then he would be prepared to press our case for grants and aids to get schemes under way.'

'You mean irrigation projects, schools?'

'Exactly. Build proper hotels. Attract tourism. Install proper sanitation. But you see my son is very young still. You will meet him. He is a bright boy. Here is his photograph taken on his thirteenth birthday last year at school in England. My husband, I tell you, was such an energetic man. But now there is nothing left for him to do. If only there were somebody vigorous and idealistic behind him, he would be a changed man, infused with new hope for the future. I don't know what plans you have, Mr Priestman, but somehow I don't see you staying a school master all your life. Think about it. Could you see your way to helping my husband prevent the sort of tragedy you stumbled upon the other day, the sort of tragedy which is happening all the time?

99

We still have some posts in our gift. The principalship of the school, for example, if you did not wish to enter a more active sphere.'

'No. What you say interests me enormously. I will certainly do what I can to interest the Maharajah, but I should have to have much more knowledge of the state, and be able to put up specific proposals if I'm to sound convincing.'

The Rani went over to a large chest, and drew from it a map of the state. For another hour, they pored together over the map, discussing present conditions and possible projects.

When Priestman left the palace, it was quite dark. Nevertheless he decided to walk back to the school to give himself time to enjoy the exhilaration he felt at the prospect of a new life full of practical hard work for the greatest good he could envisage – the alleviation of disastrous poverty and suffering. Already he foresaw details of that life, held imaginary conversations with helpers and those who obstructed him. He was no longer the interested tourist seeking sensation, or a helpless witness to suffering. And the intention to recapture something of the first three years of his life he now dismissed as trifling.

The night was pleasantly cool, and the streets crowded and noisy. Among the press of people, tongas and motorcycle rickshaws vied with buses and lorries garlanded and displaying through dirty cab windows pictures of film stars and goddesses. Merchants sat cross-legged among their wares, the Hindi and capital English letters of their shop signs large and uniform in red, yellow and black, colours repeated at the many shrines to the fierce god Hanuman, snatcher-up of Europeans. Beneath the wooden shop steps, bald pink-blotched pye dogs lay curled, their large ears attentive, their beaten eyes longing for a scrap, a kind word, a master. From every side came the blaring of radios tuned to different stations, the female singers wavering near a scream in the upper registers. And it seemed as though the entire crowd of vehicles and people and animals swayed and pulsed to the throbbing, yelling music. Yet there were areas of stillness: a man carefully burning a little pile of dried leaves and sticks at the entrance to a courtyard, the smoke slowly rising in the still air, and the acrid smell mingling with the heavy scent of joss sticks and the dry, clean aroma of maize being roasted.

As Priestman passed through all this, carefully avoiding the homeless sleeping on the pavement, he derived a new pleasure from it all. He felt a new affection for these people who would shortly come to know and trust him.

He came to a busy crossroads over which spread the branches of a large banyan tree. Its many roots were encased by a square concrete platform jutting from the edge of the pavement. Partly concealed by the lower branches was an overhead water-pipe which had sprung a bad leak. Under the gush of water stood a totally naked girl of about ten or eleven, and it surprised Priestman that she should be so unconcerned at her own nakedness among that throng of people passing below her, and that no passer-by seemed to give her a second glance. She stamped and gasped under the gushing water, rubbing her feet on the concrete to clean them, turning all the while; the light from the shop signs and the passing lurching vehicles playing over her gleaming brown body. And as she raised her arms to the water, her face was the face of ecstasy. Beside her the water spattered out on to the crisp, dry leaves lying at the base of the tree; beside her was stillness, in the dark, under the tree. 'And after her,' thought Priestman, 'it is the stillness among the dead leaves at the base of the tree that I perceive most. But I must not be distracted by the stillness there among the dead leaves where the water does not reach. It is the naked glory on the girl's face that I must concentrate on. She is poor, unknown, one of the homeless, and naked and unnoticed she stamps, and turns up her little head with joy to the gushing water.' And that was all he wanted for those other children, crawling in the dust; not a lot, no miracle of change. Just for them to turn unknown and unnoticed, reaching up their faces to the joy of the streaming water. And if any man should say to him: 'It is not your business. It is not your country', he would retort angrily that suffering knows no political boundaries, and that if any Indian came upon the suffering that existed in Priestman's country, he would expect that man to cry out in anguish, as he did now. And above all to do something, despite sneers and indifference, to do something. Then he left the girl and the tree, and made his way quickly back to the school.

When he arrived in his rooms, he swept his school books and papers off the living room table, and sat down to draft a memorandum to the Rani of their meeting. Ram Swarup, watching through the wire netting of the verandah door, saw the fierce concentration on his master's face, and quietly went back to his home.

Priestman worked long into the night, adding to the memorandum expansions of the Rani's ideas and new thoughts of his own. When he had finished typing it all in fair, he addressed an envelope to the Rani, inserted the top copy of the memorandum and the little letter to the old Rani, and went to the postbox near the dining hall where he thrust the letter in, giving the box a vigorous thump.

15

Next day, after school, Priestman asked Panwar to come to his rooms.

'My servant wants to tell me something. Please translate for me. I'm afraid I was rather short with him this morning about the money I left lying about, so I don't want any more misunderstandings. I've hidden the money, since I have nothing lockable, and I'll have to open a bank account and have next month's salary paid straight into it.'

They entered Priestman's room where Ram Swarup was waiting for them. Panwar spoke with Ram Swarup, and then turned to Priestman.

'It appears that he would like his daughter to speak English.' Panwar spoke again in a gruff voice keeping his head averted from Ram Swarup, who fawned slightly, putting his hands together and rocking his head.

'What was that about?' asked Priestman.

'These sweepers had a little school room here for their children, who cannot be taught with the children of the other servants. But the Christian who taught them had to go back to his own village. So now they haven't been to school for several years.'

'Not at all? That's appalling. Why can't they be taught with the other children?'

'They are untouchables. If they came to the servants' classes, the other children would stay away.'

'Worse and worse. You know,' continued Priestman beginning to pace the room, 'we must do something.' He smiled at Ram Swarup to excuse himself for speaking only English in his presence. 'Why can't you and I start a school for them? Perhaps just one hour a day – Hindi reading and writing from you, and some English, general knowledge and maths from me.'

'It could be done,' said Panwar looking serious. 'But other people might feel badly.'

'Who?' Panwar looked vague, and did not reply. 'You wouldn't mind doing it, would you?'

'No, it is a good idea.' He looked miserable, then plucking up courage, added: 'But why should we do it? We have so much to do as it is. This is supposed to be the Rajah's school. These fellows are rolling in money, but they are so mean, they just haven't bothered to replace the Christian teacher.'

'Well, I think you're wrong about the meanness. The government has been very hard on the Rajah financially. Anyway, can you ask Ram Swarup why he wants his daughter to learn English?'

Ram Swarup's answer was long and elaborate. 'It appears,' said Panwar, 'that he lost his only son, a boy of fifteen, from T.B. two years ago. He has transferred all his hopes for his son to his daughter. It is all very modern and unusual. But evidently the guru Agrawal thinks well of the girl. She used to listen in to the talks Mr Agrawal had with the son, who was a very serious and intelligent boy who wanted to travel like his maternal grandfather etcetera, etcetera; it goes on and on. They don't normally care about a girl's education, but I think the nub of the matter is that he thinks he will probably make a better marriage for his daughter if she knows a little English.' Panwar laughed. 'These people now want to ape upper caste customs. You know, Edward, it would be better if we were to organize something with the Junior School. We are secondary school teachers. Primary teaching is a special skill, and these children know nothing. Miss Willcox, for instance, may be willing.'

'Miss Willcox is always willing, according to you. You are unfair to the girl. I think she's rather nice. Anyway, although you may be right about special skills, I want to help. And I want to set an example, and shame the school council into action. I'm sure it's their fault, or if not, the government may well be the culprits. I think the Rani would be furious if she knew.'

'You got on well with her?'

'Yes. I think she's a splendid woman with really good ideas for progress.'

104

'Ah. She may be. But there are many others – hangers-on to the court, old uncles and such – who have very different ideas. And Percy Rajah is a pompous ass.'

'Well, it's not very nice to have your state and most of your money taken away from you, and be left with a feeling of helplessness in the face of other people's bungling. Anyway, we can't keep poor Ram Swarup hanging about. Tell him I am very sorry about his son, and that I will certainly give his daughter lessons.'

Priestman went up to Ram Swarup and patted him on the arm while Panwar translated. Ram Swarup bowed and made as if to go down and clasp Priestman's ankles.

'No, no. You must never do that!' exclaimed Priestman, jumping back. Ram Swarup straightened up and said something more.

'It appears,' said Panwar, 'that he wants a paper from you saying that she has taken lessons. These people think a piece of paper with writing on it is magic. I think he would be happier if you just gave him the piece of paper.'

'Well I'm certainly not going to hand out certificates to all and sundry. Tell him that I will give his daughter a certificate after a proper period of time, and when I'm satisfied she has made sufficient progress.'

They arranged a time when Amanti would come with her mother for her first lesson.

'Now he is asking when he can have the certificate.' Panwar spoke sternly to Ram Swarup, who quickly bowed his way backwards out of the verandah door.

'I thought caste segregation in education was against the law,' said Priestman as Panwar started to prepare the usual coffee.

'It is. But this is a very backward state.'

'Probably more backward now than in the rule of those Rajahs you hate so much.'

Panwar went into the bathroom to wash out the cups that had been beautifully cleaned by Ram Swarup.

'What are you up to chipping my cups in the basin?' called Priestman from the other room.

'There are many flies this time of year,' called back Panwar.

'Oh, you upper caste dyed-in-the-cow Brahmin gentleman,

you. Whatever am I to do with you?'

Panwar came back grinning with the cups.

'I have not died in the cow yet,' he said. 'But when I die, I can think of no better place to do it. Oh mother cow, receive me!' he cried, and plugged in the kettle. Priestman laughed loud.

'What fun we had, Panwar, you and I and Arun, those first few days! Laughing about Banglaratnam's mistake at the station. . .'

'You must go to the south!' cried Panwar. 'There is plenty of fun and sun all year round in the south, plus cheese even better than in Cheshire pubs in Throgton city.'

'Yes! And do you remember how even you eventually saw the funny side of your special effects production of *Macbeth?* And Arun with his "king lion". . . But really, what is up with Arun these days?'

'No doubt woman trouble,' said Panwar scornfully. 'Perhaps Miss Willcox is not being so willing these days. You know he is planning to move to the other end of the fort, near to Junior School.'

'No, I didn't. That will make it even more difficult for me to get him involved in the work of the English department. I will have to speak to him. Yes. All those happy first times are only ten days ago. But never mind, I am seething with new plans now. I can't tell you about them yet, but in a few weeks, after the holidays, I shall. Things are going to be very different. And I think there's a great place in all this for you, Panwar. I think I shall be able to help you a lot in your career. But first I want to experiment educating this girl of Ram Swarup's. And if I find I can communicate with her, and teach her something, then why not the others and children in the villages? You know, one of the boys at least has the right idea. He's teaching his lifelong untouchable friend to read. I haven't seen him here so much since his friend came, but there's an example for us all.'

'Who is this boy?' asked Panwar, handing Priestman his coffee.

'Oh, Ashok something; you know him. I think he was in *Macbeth.'* Panwar turned quickly, and went back to busy himself with the coffee things. He drew in breath, swallowed, and his hands shook.

'Hey!' cried Priestman. 'Stop chipping my cups again. They're not so untouchable you have to break them. Yes, and I must start Hindi lessons with Mr Mattacharya.'

'Contraction of Hindi section of School Review is so constant, it will become minus Hindi section,' said Panwar in Mattacharya's accent. But there was no mirth in his joke, and he kept his face averted.

'And on Sunday, m' boy, you and I are going to find that village. And that will show them. I've had about enough of their nonsense. Block Officers indeed!'

The old Rani lay in bed while her daughter-in-law read to her for the fourth time the letter from the 'Viceroy'.

'Isn't that marvellous news, mother-in-law? Now you can stop worrying.'

'I worry even more,' said the old Rani, and smiled grimly.

'Why? Surely it's a splendid letter?'

'A splendid fake,' said the old Rani with satisfaction. ' "Her Imperial Majesty", indeed! Do they think I'm completely senile? Why! Everybody knows Queen Victoria is dead.'

'No, no. They mean Queen Elizabeth.'

'Don't be ridiculous. She died with the Spanish Armada.'

'No. The Second, mother-in-law.'

'Exactly. The Second George. The first one died in 1936. George the Second is on the throne. You can't fool me. I know my genealogies. And the English are up to something. This will not help poor Percy. He must not be told. He will worry so. Fetch me the prime minister. Go, go, child!'

16

There are some mornings that throw the beholder out of his present life. The freshness of the air, the clarity with which each far brick and leaf is seen, and above all the long-forgotten scents which assail him, combine to cast him back to the mornings of childhood when entering a garden it seemed the day could never end.

So it was for Priestman that Sunday morning as he made his way with Panwar down from the fort to the town and the bicycle shop. He sucked the air through his teeth the better to savour it. The Indian winter's morning was like the best day of an English summer. On just such a morning his mother had thrown open his bedroom curtains and declared: 'Another gorgeous day. The picnic will definitely take place!' And to Priestman, remembrance of the past gave to the future an almost ferociously vigorous promise, for on such a day all things seemed possible.

'You know,' Priestman remarked to Panwar, 'human feelings can be so fraudulent. Here we are embarking upon a mission of mercy, a matter of life and death. There should be a set to my jaw and a furrow to my brow, yet all I feel like doing is bursting into song and turning a somersault. Have you ever played leapfrog? No of course you haven't. Well come and lose some of that fat.' And they progressed through the Monkey Gate and down the road, taking it in turn to leapfrog over each other. Squirrels bounded up trees, clinging half-way up to watch them. An old priest, surrounded by dusty-smelling marigolds at a little whitewashed temple carved out of the cliff, eyed them carefully, though neither with approval nor disapproval for the antics of humanity had long since ceased to affect him.

Panting and laughing, they stopped their game to look up, blinking at the bands of mosaic tiles on the walls of the fortress.

The enamelled eyes of ducks, peacocks and elephants sharply reflected the light, and seemed to wink down at them.

A group of gaily dressed women in holiday mood passed them laughing and laden with frangipani blossom, thick-scented, and the delicate jasmin – offerings for the temple.

Panwar began to sing: *'woh chale haa woh chale hi woh chale jhatak ke daman. . .'* So singing, he danced down the hill, swaying his wide hips in imitation of the women, and beckoning seductively to Priestman who followed him roaring with laughter.

Priestman and Panwar arrived before the girls, as agreed, at the bicycle shop. They arranged the hire to their satisfaction, then wandered next door to a bookshop. Priestman was amazed at the brightness of its window display compared to that of practically every other shop in the town, and at the wares displayed. They were almost wholly Communist revolutionary literature; blood-red dust-jackets covered with stars and proletarian implements, among which burst forth raised fists and forward-looking gentlemen with narrow eyes.

When they entered the shop, its only occupant, the owner, completely ignored them. Priestman was rather put out by this attitude, so used had he become in such a short time to immediate deference. Panwar knew the man slightly, having ordered from him books for the school library. Priestman was somewhat heartened to see that the shelves contained many standard works of world literature, including the same editions of Dostoievsky, Tolstoy and Chekhov as those which adorned the Rani's sitting room. There were also text-books on many subjects. He assumed that an embassy or two were paying for the facility of the window display. While browsing, Panwar asked some question to which the owner replied with civility and intelligence, though scarcely bothering to look up. Panwar went outside for the second time to see if the girls had arrived, since they had arranged to meet at ten o'clock and it was now quarter past.

They did not arrive until nearly half past, and though Priestman tried to hide his irritation, something about the bookshop and its owner's manner had changed his earlier mood. The revolutionary figures on the dust-covers had reminded him of that other world which was active even in this backwater, and whose columns stood poised, fists raised in unison, not far to the north. This time, thought Priestman, Tamburlaine's descendant would not turn at little Karatpore to cry out: 'We venture no further into such an inhospitable land.' His irritation was increased because the women had arrived equipped in attitude and attire more for a picnic than for a serious expedition.

Miss Willcox was in jolly mood. She sported a wide-brimmed straw hat, dyed purple at the crown and having a fringe of loose straw through which she peered and which she continuously attempted to brush aside, for all the world as if fresh from a romp in a haystack. A black bra showed through her shocking pink blouse. She wore a pair of tightly-fitting, bright green trousers of a metallic dazzling hue more suitable for the body-work of a sports car. The whole effect was not improved by the tightness of the trousers at her ankles, nor by a pair of black high-heeled shoes with wide straps. The hat in particular seemed to amuse Panwar out of all proportion. Priestman had to frown at him to stop his continuous grin. The nurse was conventionally dressed in white Punjabi trousers, tunic and scarf. But it appeared that she had brought the minimum of medical supplies; a depleted first-aid kit which in addition to some antiseptic, a small bottle of aspirin, bandages and cotton wool was found to contain, on Priestman's examination, a tin of sticking plasters from which the contents had disappeared save for six of the narrowest strips. The nurse seemed ill at ease, and addressed her few remarks only to Miss Willcox.

There then followed a deal of haggling about the bicycles, which the women declared unfit to ride. Eventually, superior models were procured from the back of the shop. A much higher deposit had to be laid down. A further half hour was lost with all these dealings. It then transpired that although the nurse knew how to ride, Miss Willcox had not been on a bicycle since her early convent days. She said that the nuns had frowned upon the practice, but that being a sporting girl, always in trouble with the mother superior, she had had the gardener teach her.

'The nuns caught us. And I sailed straight into a barbed wire fence. I was lucky not to be scarred for life!' It appeared that the gardener was steadying the twelve-year-old Miss Willcox in a

110

manner disapproved of by the nuns. 'He was dismissed!' cried Miss Willcox, mounting the machine, 'just because he had one hand on the small of my back.' Priestman eyed the small of her back, wondering whether he was expected to follow the gardener as her mentor.

'And his other hand?' enquired Panwar blandly.

'History does not record,' said Miss Willcox, and frowning at the wobbling handlebars, she raised a cautious foot to the pedal. The nurse came to her assistance. Miss Willcox wobbled, nearly came off several times, and expressed alarm and amusement by turns.

After a further ten minutes, the little expedition started on its way, accompanied for a while by children of all ages who had gathered round to laugh and make ribald remarks. There were frequent stops for rest, and every time they came to the slightest gradient, the men had to get off and help push the women's bikes.

'What a glorious day, Mr Priestman!' cried Miss Willcox as he pushed her machine up the hill. 'What a pity we could not have gone to the dam, and picnicked by the falling water.'

'Another day we shall,' said Priestman. She gave him a broad sideways smile.

A fork in the road caused delay. Priestman had assumed that Panwar knew the way. But he had only the vaguest notion. They had to wait for twenty minutes till a man driving a bullock cart directed them. After a further half hour, they stopped speaking to each other. The heat was growing, and the brightness of the morning had given way to haze. There was no shade. Far to their right, a spiral of dust slowly crossed the parched fields like some giant gastropod. The nurse pulled the scarf over her head, and Panwar made great play of retrieving Miss Willcox's hat pretending that it was a chicken, clucking at it, and bringing it back on the end of a stick. Miss Willcox grabbed the hat irritably, and the nurse allowed herself one of her few smiles. Priestman watched them amused, following the patterns of emotion between them all. Threads of irritability, jealousy, disdain, expectancy, fear, pride and lust joined them, and were tugged or slackened at each look, each movement, every gust of wind or pothole.

'Panwar,' said Priestman at the next bend, 'I don't want to ride into Bhonsa. I don't want them to know we are here. Would you ride on ahead so that we shan't come across the village suddenly, and signal us to stop when you see it?'

Panwar stopped on the brow of a hill, and waved to them not to come forward. They dismounted, all glad that the hill did not have to be negotiated. Panwar returned to say that the village was in sight. The girls were for stopping and refreshing themselves by the roadside under a clump of palms, but Priestman insisted that they get off the road to avoid being seen.

It proved very difficult to wheel the bicycles over the rough ground, and the girls grumbled considerably. In spite of her high heels, Miss Willcox managed rather better than the nurse who did not complain so much as sigh, look sick and stumble.

'I shall definitely pay for this tomorrow, Mr Priestman,' muttered Miss Willcox, wagging a finger at him. 'You have a lot to answer for, naughty man.'

'Ha,' said Priestman, not appreciating this sort of banter. 'You must keep fit to perform your role of chaperone adequately.'

'Perhaps,' said Panwar, 'the chaperone is being chaperoned, and the hunter hunted.'

'Obscure,' answered Priestman. 'Some lost Restoration comedy no doubt?'

Suddenly, the nurse sat down, and began to wave her head from side to side like a shot giraffe. It was apparent that she could go no further for the time being. Priestman went forward a few yards, and came back to say that there was a *nullah* ahead. They continued to it, Miss Willcox supporting the nurse, who refused offers of help from the men. In the *nullah* they took shelter from the sun under an overhanging bank hollowed out by the monsoon floods. Here they had lunch. But the aches and pains complained of by the girls, and the fact that the meal was frugal since each party thought the other would have provided the bulk of it, did little to restore their spirits. There was nothing to see save the opposite side of the *nullah,* and after a while even Miss Willcox stopped discoursing on the beauty of the dam they should have visited.

Priestman considered what a mistake it had all been, and how badly he had planned it. He imagined that Panwar had taken care of the details, but of course he was against the expedition because the women had been invited. Priestman was angry that he felt the constant urge to apologize to them.

'Well, I'm sorry that this isn't the ideal picnic,' said Priestman firmly. 'But it wasn't intended to be. Our purpose is not entirely amusement, as I think you know. So if you're all quite finished, I think we had better get started and find that village.'

'Of course,' said Miss Willcox, looking serious. 'Poor us have so little opportunity for relaxation that we seize at any straw. Yes, you are quite right, we must press on.'

'What is the point?' said the nurse, uttering her first full sentence of the day.

The others looked quickly at Priestman who had gone very red. He said nothing for a moment.

'I see. Well. Of course. Alright then.' Priestman frowned, trying to keep his temper, and wondering how he could make the best of this turn of events. Perhaps Arun Sen had been right about the profession of nurse in this country. But then the profession of school teacher was not considered so highly either. Salary and saintliness counted for more.

'Miss Willcox, are you coming?' asked Priestman.

'Of course, I would have been delighted. But I cannot really leave her.'

'I suppose not. Panwar, you're very silent. What do you think?'

'I would come with you, but that would leave the two ladies alone.'

'That's logical, if nothing else. So it looks as though I shall have to go alone. Though I must say the object of this exercise was to have witnesses to prove that I wasn't mad or something.'

'You could bring us to the village if you find it,' said Panwar.

'But think, half an hour there, half an hour to come back, half an hour to return with you. Well alright, but it's quite likely I shall lose my way or something on one of those journeys.'

'I could come with you,' Miss Willcox piped up.

'That's marvellous. But is it allowed?'

'Why should we bother our heads all the time with what is allowed or not allowed? The purpose of this mission is much more important. We would never do anything important if it had to be allowed first.'

The nurse snorted, and raised her eyes to the sky.

'Great!' said Priestman with energy. 'And you two will be alright alone here?'

'Oh, yes. Very good,' said Panwar unhappily. The nurse hunched her back against the side of the hollow and looked away. Then she glanced back angrily at Miss Willcox, who was struggling to rise, and was given a helping hand by Priestman. Miss Willcox, still supported by Priestman's hand, hobbled the first few steps.

Priestman looked back at the two left behind. Panwar had stood up and was walking about prodding hard lumps of earth with his shoe. The sun had now moved so that there was barely any shade in the little hollow. The nurse lay back, and covered her face with her scarf.

'How kind you are,' smiled Miss Willcox. 'I think I am alright now. I have quite regained my sea legs.' They went over a little rise and were lost to view by the others.

Because Priestman did not want to go near the village of Bhonsa, he made more of a detour than was strictly necessary. They entered another *nullah*, which Priestman calculated would lead to the buffalo pool. For a moment he left the girl in the *nullah*, while he climbed its side, hoping that he would catch a glimpse of Bhonsa, and so get his bearings. But the village was not visible. He returned to her smiling, grateful for her companionship and conscious of the effort she was making on his behalf, and all the time worried that he would not be able to locate the lost village, yet appalled at the thought of what he would find there if he did.

'I'm sorry to drag you into all this,' he said as they continued down the watercourse. 'Now I think of it, I can't understand why I just didn't hire a taxi one afternoon and come out by myself or with Panwar. Of course, I didn't know till Tuesday evening that the authorities had been unable to find the place. Still the delay is unforgivable. But people have been putting so many doubts into my mind. Oh, well.'

'You take too much upon yourself. I hear you are working so hard at the school too. You must not blame yourself.'

'You see, the English of the boys taking public examinations is

114

in an absolute mess. And it's affecting all their other subjects. It really is a full-time job sorting it all out. Macgregor has been gone a year, I gather, and he wasn't much use in his last year. I spend most of my time telling them I'm not Macgregor. "Mr Macgregor took classes out of doors in winter, sir. Mr Macgregor let us pick berries by the battlements, sir. Did you know Mr Macgregor sir?" Well, that's enough of that.'

'You cannot hope to sort out such muddles in five minutes. And I expect you do not get too much help from some people in your department?'

'They'll come round. Mind you, when the school doesn't give its staff proper food and accommodation, it's hard to instil great enthusiasm. And I distrust new brooms, so I don't want to go charging around altering everything blindly.'

'Though you would like to.'

'A lot of the time. But come on, we must concentrate on where we are going, or I shall make a mess of this expedition too.' Then he became more animated, thinking that he recognized the now much steeper sides of the *nullah,* and a sharp turn to the right in its direction. 'You know, I'm a fool. The place would be visible from the air. That's the answer. And we have our splendid Rajah with his little spotter plane. Why isn't my brain working properly, tell me?'

'There is so much new to you, and you have not been well.'

'My precious health!'

'And the Rajah may not be willing.'

'Oh, Miss Willcox, he may not be willing. That is true.'

'We need not be too formal now. My name is Sheila.'

'How are you Sheila? My name's Edward.' He shook her hand, and they both laughed. 'The trouble with me, Sheila, is that I cannot stay gloomy for long. I sometimes think something is seriously wrong with me. Even this morning coming down from the school, I fooled about on the road. You know that old pessimistic saying, "in the midst of life we are in death" or something like that, well it's as though my motto were "in the midst of death we are in life".'

'I think that basically you are a very happy person, Edward, and were not ready for the sight of great poverty. Besides, you are young and full of life.' She smiled at him to indicate that she too was young and full of life.

'Yes, I suppose. But I'm twenty-nine. At what age does one become ready for the sight of great poverty? But wait a minute. Yes. I'm sure we're on the right track. If I'm not much mistaken we should reach the pool soon. If the girls are there, they can take us to the village.'

'What girls?'

'Just two little girls with their buffalo. You'll have to speak to them. They're scared of me.'

'If only we did not have that long ride back.' She trailed behind him, stumbling from time to time in an effort to catch up. Priestman turned to her excitedly.

'Look, the pool. Now we're getting somewhere. The girls aren't here, but I'm sure it's the same place. Look at the holes made by the animal's hooves. Of course, the water has gone down a bit.' Miss Willcox hobbled up to the pool and surveyed it without enthusiasm.

'There will be several such pools at this time of year. I have often seen this sort of pool. Each one will be used by buffaloes. Are you sure it is the same?'

'Well, not absolutely. But fairly certain. Anyway, if I'm right, the village can't be more than fifteen minutes away. All we have to do is follow the tracks of the buffalo.'

'And you are sure the girls came from the village? Were they undernourished?'

'No. Not particularly. Anyway I'm pretty sure that that's the path to the village.'

'Edward. I am sorry. I am so fagged out, really. Why don't you run on to the village, and I will wait here. I shall be alright.' She eased herself down to a sitting position.

'If you're sure you'll be alright?'

'Yes, yes. But come back soon.'

'Yes, I will.' Priestman set off at a run up the path. The way seemed right. Occasionally he came across buffalo dung and hoof prints. After a hundred yards, he slowed to a walk. Although signs of the buffalo had given out, he was still confident of being on the right track, and began to prepare himself for the ordeal of meeting the villagers. He began to convince himself that the village would appear round every

116

bend, and each time he came to one, he steeled himself for the sight of it. On turning yet another bend, he came to another buffalo wallow at the joining of two large dried watercourses and a smaller third. He climbed the steepest bank to get his bearings, but the ground around him was higher than the bank, and he could see no sign of habitation.

'Fool. Fool. Idiot!' he cried aloud. 'Oh for Theseus' thread! Oh, for a helicopter!' And all the time he was conscious of the woman waiting alone, worried, by the pool. 'What does she want of me? A triumph, romance, sex, distraction, love, marriage? I could wander in circles for an eternity in this place. No, I shall not give up. Stage two will be the aeroplane. If we can't find them from a plane, then I am, or was, mad. "Yes, of course, your Highness, I love small aircraft. Another thing, your Highness, these villagers had gold and precious jewels. No use for them. Strange, eh what? Probably belonged to you in the first place. Mountains of it." That's the way. Anything to get him up and searching. He'll come like a shot, poor Percy.' He hurriedly retraced his steps, elated by his new plan, and anxious to get back and put it into practice.

'Hi there!' he yelled catching sight of Miss Willcox still sitting by the pool. 'Sorry I've been so long.' He pulled her up with both hands and swung her round.

'You are in a very happy mood?' she laughed. 'You have found the village and they are not starving.'

'No. Impossible. This was all wrong. I'm sorry to have brought you on such a fruitless search. But now I know the sure way to do it, my dear splendid, helpful girl. But first I'm going to have a swim. So you had better look the other way, 'cos I'm going to plunge naked right into that lovely cool water.'

'You cannot do it. No, please don't pooh-pooh me. The water is filthy, you do not know what germs there may be.'

'Oh, pooh, pooh and double pooh.' He began to unbutton his shirt. You're not going to join me? Very well then, off you go!' He shooed her away, and she backed a few paces, watching him as he stripped off his shirt.

'But if anyone should come?'

'So? You will tell them you are my sister guarding my clothes, and they are to go away.'

She continued to stare at him as though he were some strange creature.

'Well,' he continued, starting to undo his trousers, 'if you're not going, I don't mind. I'm not ashamed of being seen naked.' She took another step back, and half turned away.

'Promise me you will not swallow any water.'

'No. That's sensible. I shan't. You're very thoughtful.' He was naked now, and he put forward a hand and pressed her shoulder. The muscles in her arm jumped as though burnt, but she stood her ground. 'In England we would think nothing of bathing naked like this.'

'This is not England.' He held her head and turned it gently towards his mouth. Her head moved stiffly in little jerks as though it were on a ratchet.

'Not here. Not yet,' she said. 'If anyone should come.' He quickly bent and kissed her temple. Then with a shout, he turned, ran and plunged into the pool. He splashed and turned rolling over and over in the shallow water. She bent and gathering up his scattered clothes, moved with them a little way off, and sat down, her head averted.

'*Aré, aré!*' he shouted, pretending to slap a lazy buffalo. Then he was a porpoise bucking through the water. She could not avoid watching him.

He stumbled out of the water, and began to do exercises.

'Up, two, three. Down, two, three. You should do this one. Good for the tummy muscles. God! I feel fit! One day soon, we'll go to your dam. Then you can swim too.'

'I don't swim.' She had turned now and was watching him without trying to conceal the fact. But watching him as though he were some sort of show, unconnected with her in any way.

'Well, I'll teach you. And I'll teach you to dive too.' He ran to her, and standing before her, raised both her arms above her head, and pushed her head down to the diving position. Then he lifted her straight up, then down again, then up and down again. And all the time she looked into his face with an impassive but enquiring expression as if to say: 'What will you do next?' Her hat had fallen to the ground. Stepping back a few paces, he picked it up and threw it to her like a frisbee. 'Come on, throw it back.'

She tried, but her throw was clumsy, and the hat sailed into the middle of the pool where it sat, its fringe and purple crown looking very much out of place on the muddy water. He went to the pool to retrieve it.

They both saw the others coming at about the same time.

'Hi!' yelled Priestman waving cheerily at them. 'Just going to get the mud off, and retrieve the hat, then I'll be with you.'

The nurse walked quickly down the slope, and came up to Miss Willcox.

'You have mud on your fat face, Sheila Willcox,' said the nurse. 'Here, let me wipe it off for you.' She put out a hand to Miss Willcox's face, then pushed it hard so that Miss Willcox staggered and fell. Then the nurse sat down, and began to retch and cry. Miss Willcox sat where she had fallen, staring at the nurse, then she put her head in her hands. Panwar quickly gathered up Priestman's clothes, and brought them to the edge of the pool.

'This water is very dirty,' said Panwar. 'And now you run the risk of a chill.' He handed Priestman his clothes. 'Edward, was this wise?'

'Yes. Extremely bloody wise!' He pulled on his trousers and went over to the sobbing women.

'Why the hell did you hit her, you stupid bitch? Nothing happened, if that's what you think. We were just enjoying ourselves, having fun for a change.'

'Oh yes. We saw your fun, saw it all, very nice!' replied the nurse shrilly.

'No you didn't. You missed the earlier rape scene. What about Bombay, then? Where's your address? Come on, write it down. I don't know why you came on this trip. If you're so ill, see a doctor.'

'Edward, I think that is enough now,' said Panwar. 'You do not really understand our customs.'

'No I don't. But does that mean I have to behave like you all the time?'

'This is not England, Edward.'

'So I've heard.'

'I do not think that even in the UK you would behave quite like this.'

'Well, to hell with it.' He tugged on his shirt. 'Come on Sheila Willcox, do get up. She didn't exactly pole-axe you.' He reached for her hand, but she brushed his away.

'Don't touch me!'

'Alright. But do stop play-acting. I didn't exactly ask you to stand gawping at me. Let's go, for heaven's sake!'

Each walked separately back to the bicycles.

'I thought we agreed not to leave the bikes unattended,' said Priestman.

'The blind *saddhu* came up,' said Panwar. 'He asked for you. We gave him money, but he would not go away. The nurse began to get hysterical because of his presence. She was very distressed. Then we heard your shouting in the pool, so we came and found you. I do not think, Edward, that you were looking too seriously for that village.'

'I was. I didn't find it. But I will. And stop bugging me.'

When they arrived at the bikes, the beggar had gone. They mounted and cycled away. After half a mile, a car came along. The women waved it down, threw their bikes in the ditch, and hitched a lift. Awkwardly pushing the abandoned bikes, Priestman and Panwar continued cycling.

'You know, Edward, that these women will spread rumours to your disadvantage. They will think we will talk about what happened, and each will think the other will try to discredit her, so they will both want to get in their versions first. Miss Willcox will say something to Arun Sen. He would believe anything he wanted to believe, then pass it on as fact. I should have warned you, Edward, these people make out they are your friends, and oh so modern, but they are not very nice. I am sorry you have got mixed up with them. It is my fault.'

'Oh nonsense,' sighed Priestman. 'I suppose I've made a great mess of things.'

'No, no. I would say just an average middle-of-the-road-style mess-up. But you are so well thought of that even if there are rumours, it will probably not matter.'

'You really are my friend, aren't you, Panwar?'

'You should not need to ask.'

'I don't. And now we shall have a middle-of-the-road average style mess-up.' So saying, he drove his two bicycles into

120

Panwar's, so that both men staggered and fell off laughing into a tangle of turning wheels and twisted handlebars.

At the pool, the blind beggar stood, turning in half circles as though testing the wind. Miss Willcox's straw hat floated in the water. Now only its purple crown showed above the surface.

Some time after the beggar had gone, the two naked little girls arrived with their buffalo. The buffalo nuzzled the hat with his soft whiskery lips. The elder girl picked it up and put it on the animal's head. They both laughed at the sight, and the beast turned his head and shot out his tongue affectionately at the small girl on his back. The hat fell off. The elder girl put it on her head and performed a dance along the margin of the pool, singing, '*cha, chicky cha, chicky cha*'.

17

'Arun, we are far too shaken to speak,' said Miss Willcox, seating herself heavily on the couch in the little room near the Junior School. 'You see Sunita. She is practically passing out all the time.'

'Some brandy?' asked Arun, going to the dressing table drawer.

'How can you remain so calm? We must immobilize Priestman before he destroys us all. He is mad. He practically raped me. Poor Sunita saw it all, and thought I was encouraging him. But now she understands, poor dear.' The poor dear, who was lying on the couch, nodded as Miss Willcox stroked her hair. 'You should wear it short, my dear, in this dreadful climate. I really think she should receive medical attention.' They took the proffered brandy.

Arun Sen seated himself at the table, and drummed his fingers upon it while smiling at Miss Willcox. 'Of course, Sheila, he is very free-thinking and Protestant. It was, I am afraid to say, to be expected. He is not really the type you should mix with. Such people would not have gentle passion for you; it would not be beautiful.' He placed his hand on the Khajuraho book.

'And how he abused Sunita! I have never heard such a scream of abuse.'

'And did not Panwar intervene to protect you?'

'That thing? What could that half man do?'

'If only I had been there to protect you both, none of this would have happened.'

'Yes, yes. But now we must act to protect our good name. We beg you to act.'

'And if I act, will I be restored to your favours?'

'Yes, yes.' The nurse too nodded her assent.

122

'You would both together show your gratitude?'

'What would you do?' The women smiled at one another.

'Many things. You will leave all that to me. And you will agree to give lessons here to one or two of the servant girls? Yes? Then it is settled.'

'It is settled. But you must act fast before rumours spread.'

Soon after this conversation, Priestman went to the principal's bungalow. The principal asked how he had spent his day.

'I have done something un-Indian and caused offence,' said Priestman, pursing his lips and giving a strained smile.

'Impossible!'

'I'm afraid so. I went on a cycle trip with Panwar, the nurse and Miss Willcox. The aim was to find the village. That was the reason for taking the nurse. And she would not come without a chaperone. That is the reason for Miss Willcox. I went off alone to find the village. I could not. On the way back, I bathed in a pool. The girls came across me by accident. I made a silly joke that they should join me. They were insulted, it appears. They hitched a lift back. I am to blame, and I have acted foolishly.'

'This is terrible!' cried the principal. 'What sort of water was it?'

'A buffalo pool.'

'We must get you injections. Why did you not say you wanted to bathe? There is a proper filtered and chlorinated swimming-pool in the town, at the brick factory. And why did the women not turn their backs and go away?'

'They did. But they were offended.'

'They should not have agreed to come. Panwar should have stopped this mad venture. He should have told you that this is not the way we do things. By now these women will have spread rumours all over the fort.'

'I can't see that Panwar is to blame. He was not at all happy with the whole thing. I persuaded him against his better judgement.'

'No, no. He should have told me what you proposed. He is a silly young man. And these women; they are very much to blame.'

'Well, I hardly think that's fair, sir. I invited them. They accepted. It was in a good cause.' Priestman frowned at the lameness of the phrase 'in a good cause' to describe the purpose of the expedition.

'No, my dear Edward, you do not understand.' The principal leant forward, a hand on each knee. 'They are very loose. Very difficult. I am sorry you have got mixed up with them. It is my fault, I should have warned you. But then you come so seldom to see me in the evenings. We have never really had the chance to get to know each other.' Priestman sighed and muttered about being busy. He found the principal a little difficult to take; his manner alternated so much between the very smooth and the suddenly dictatorial.

'I'm sorry. But I must repeat that nobody is to blame but myself.'

The principal laughed, throwing up his head. He stood up, crossed over to Priestman and patted him on the shoulder. 'My dear Edward, you must not think of such a thing; not talk of such a thing. You are so English, so honest. You mean no harm. But why did you not believe me when I said there was no village? There was such an extensive search. Anyway, never mind. Whose car was it?'

'I'm sorry? Oh, the car that picked up the girls. I don't know.'

'Alright. Now listen to me please. You must say nothing of this matter to anybody. I will see to everything. Go back to your rooms now, please. I will arrange it all.' Priestman got up to leave. 'And Edward. You must throw all this nonsense of a village out of your head. I don't know what there is there. I do not care. You are not responsible for these people. Neither am I. Please promise me never to go there again.'

'Once again, my apologies,' said Priestman as he left. 'I understand.' But he promised nothing.

That evening Miss Willcox and the nurse were called to the principal's office and dismissed. They left the fort later that night, and were driven down to the station.

Panwar was also called to the principal, and afterwards he came to Priestman's rooms and told him the news. It appeared that Panwar had been very severely reprimanded, and told that if he made one further mistake, he would lose his job.

Angrily Priestman accompanied him back to the principal's bungalow.

'Really, Edward,' said the principal frowning, 'I would rather you forgot the matter. It has been dealt with. It is at an end.'

'I would like to know, sir, what you intend for Mr Panwar since he is a very valuable and trusted member of my department, and I could not continue without him. And really, I cannot understand why these women have been dismissed.'

The principal was tired and ready for bed. He turned angrily on Panwar, and berated him, mostly in Hindi.

'I agree, sir,' said Panwar with dignity, 'that it was a mistake to involve the ladies.'

'Ladies, ladies you say. What is this talk of ladies?'

'Yes sir, it was a mistake to involve them, and I persuaded them against their better judgement to go.'

'There is so much nobility in the English department tonight,' sighed the principal, raising his hands. 'If only it was matched with more discretion.'

'I agree sir,' continued Panwar sadly. 'But may I point out that the purpose of this trip was to find and relieve poor, starving people.'

'Not again, please!' said the principal throwing his head back in exasperation, and banging one arm on his chair. 'All that is under the bridge.' He raised his arm, fingers together, and brought it down, fingers apart, in a gesture which indicated that the subject was closed. He looked at Priestman for confirmation, but the latter rocked his head to one side which signified agreement to the Indian, but for Priestman meant that he would not commit himself.

'The trip was not for the purpose of some lewd assignation,' continued Panwar, who had evidently found his tongue because of Priestman's presence and initial support. Priestman had never heard Panwar argue so calmly before. 'That it all went wrong because Mr Priestman, an Englishman and our guest, felt naturally hot and in need of a swim, is not the issue. Did not Gandhi teach us to care for the poor? They have not been mentioned in all this talk, which is of reputations and other secondary matters.'

'Please do not bring the name of Gandhi into this. I will not allow it! And now I am the villain. Not caring for the poor. Have I not made endless efforts to find out the truth of Edward's claim?' The principal opened his arms wide in appeal to Priestman, who opened his hands in answer and apparent agreement. It seemed to him as though for once Panwar was in command.

'Principal Sahib,' continued Panwar, speaking very calmly as though instructing his superior. 'You have done your best. But we know how authority can be corrupt, muddled, or just lazy. We cannot always abide by what authority tells us. And Edward, quite rightly, wished to be sure.'

'Panwar,' said Priestman, 'you have said my piece much better than I could have done. I'm very impressed, and very grateful.'

'Of course, I shall resign, sir,' continued Panwar, ignoring Priestman, 'since that will save you the embarrassment of dismissing me at the next opportunity. I shall leave tonight. But I shall not leave the district. I do not think you are quite empowered to make me do that. I will make my own enquiries into this matter until I am satisfied one way or the other. And as you know, my father is a headmaster, though not of such a grand Rajah's school as this. I shall ask him to help find these two unfortunate women a job or at least provide them with proper references.' Panwar got up, and placing a hand on Priestman's shoulder added, 'I am better able than you to get to the truth of this village matter. I will write. Goodnight. Goodnight, sir.'

Priestman stood up and addressed the principal. 'Sir, if Panwar resigns or is dismissed, I shall resign. Indeed, in view of the fact that these women have got the sack, I resign now anyway.'

The principal let out a little howl, and buried his head briefly in his hands. He cried out to a servant from whom he ordered coffee and a beer for Priestman.

'Sit down, I beg you. Sit down both of you. What is all this talk of resignations? I have never mentioned resignations. Mr Panwar, I had no idea you felt so strongly about these matters.'

'Nor did I, sir,' replied Panwar, 'until I started talking about them.' They all laughed a little.

'Well,' continued the principal, 'this is a pretty kettle of fish. You have caught me on a sticky wicket, eh Edward?'

'Sir,' said Priestman, sipping his beer and wishing it was whisky, 'I must really ask you to reinstate those girls.'

'Edward, you do not understand. This is not the first time these women have caused difficulties. This was simply the last straw. Your predecessor, Mr Macgregor. . . Well, I would rather not go into all that. It is too painful for me.' He sighed and hunched his back. 'The burdens of this job. I am no longer young. I stay on here because I love my job. The school has been all my life. My only life. Is Banglaratnam fit to succeed me? I had hoped. . . No, these women were not good. All I would ask is to retire here. I would give up the principalship and all this wretched administration, and just stay on doing a little teaching which now I have no time for. I am a teacher, that is what I love. Would it work, do you think?'

'I'm afraid,' said Priestman, 'that unless the new principal were a very confident and understanding man, he would be nervously looking over his shoulder all the time at you. But come, all that is far off. You seem very fit and sprightly to me.'

'I am sixty-five,' said the principal as though seeking approval.

'No!' said Priestman incredulously, feeling sorry for the man.

'Yes,' continued the principal brightening up. 'There is something about the air of the fort which keeps one's health. Mrs Bhoshi is well into her seventies and still teaching.'

'I long to meet her. Oh dear,' sighed Priestman. 'Poor Miss Willcox. Really, can nothing be done?'

They went round the matter for a long time, but the principal was adamant that the women could not be reinstated. However, he finally agreed that they should be sent good references, and that Panwar's father would see if he could help. But underneath all this talk, there developed between the three of them a tacit agreement that perhaps after all the two women were not ideal, and any help they gave was in the manner of charity, and that they were exceeding the bounds of what was necessary. Priestman stopped pressing the matter as he began to feel relief that the women had left. However, he did press the question of the village. It was finally agreed that the Rajah should be approached for the use of his plane, that Priestman should fly over the area as a passenger, and that if they failed to locate the village, the matter would be at an end.

Then they talked of things generally, of the School Review, of examination prospects and so on.

'You know,' sighed Priestman, 'if I had gone to Bhonsa in a hired car by myself, all this could have been avoided.'

'I would have lent you mine, if you had told me,' said the principal. 'But I'm afraid it's on the blink again. This new driver knows nothing, and it is practically impossible to get repairs in the town. Spare parts are so hard to come by, and so expensive.'

'You know it's exactly the same model as the one I sold before coming here. Would you like me to have a look at it?' said Priestman eagerly.

'Would you? Really Edward, you are amazing. So much talent. If you get it to work, you may drive it whenever you want. I will give you the spare keys.'

When Priestman, together with Panwar, came to the steps of his room, he found Ram Swarup waiting for him.

'Oh, blast it!' cried Priestman. 'It was his daughter's first lesson this evening. I completely forgot. Please tell him that I will see her tomorrow after school.' Panwar did so, and Ram Swarup went away apparently happy. 'Now that's something I can really put my mind to. It will be very interesting. I haven't taught a girl before either. I've seen her briefly. She's a nice child. Good-looking too. Alright, you wouldn't think so. Too dark for you.'

'Really, Edward, I wish you had let me resign.'

'I would not dream of losing you. You're the only help I've really got. You're a splendid teacher, and a very good man. Won't you come in for a while?' Priestman looked at him, worried.

'You must not say such things. I am not those things you think. I am not fit to be a teacher.' And so saying, he hurried off into the dark.

18

The following afternoon, Priestman devoted the hour after
school before Amanti's first lesson to inspecting the principal's
car. It was kept in a lean-to shed beside Priestman's quarters. Its
driver was a cheerful lad who explained that he had been
engaged as a driver not as a mechanic, but that he was very
willing to learn. He had an eager face which looked well with a
smear of engine oil on one cheek.

The car Priestman had sold was blue, whereas the principal's
was green, but in most other respects they were very similar.
Priestman had sold his car with regret, so now it was with a smile
of recognition that he ran his hand over the familiar contours of
the bodywork, fiddled with the controls, and examined the
engine and under-bonnet components which were covered with
grease topped by a thick layer of dust.

'Phwoof!' exclaimed the driver, screwing up his face and
spitting out imaginary particles of grit. Priestman agreed that
dust was probably a major cause of the trouble. They spent a
contented hour dismantling filters, cleaning sparking plugs, and
checking the timing mechanism. Priestman was happy to be
using his hands again. Then he briefly drove the car up and down
in front of his quarters to the cheers of the boys. There was still a
deal of spluttering and loss of power, which sounded to
Priestman like gasket trouble. It was agreed that next day they
would take off the cylinder head.

After Priestman had showered and entered his living room,
Ram Swarup came through the verandah door. He was followed
by his wife, and then by Amanti. The mother came in at a
crouching run, hiding her face. Ignoring Priestman's 'good
evening, Mrs Swarup', she rushed to the wall beside the door and

squatted down. Ram Swarup hovered in an anguish of embarrassment. Only Amanti seemed to remain calm. Sometimes she frowned, sometimes smiled briefly, but she remained standing a few paces within the door while her father constantly pointed her out as though he were a salesman.

'Alright,' said Priestman. 'Go and sit over there, Ram Swarup.' Ram Swarup looked behind him in despair, not knowing what was expected of him. Then his wife shattered the silence with a short sentence from behind the cloth over her face. Ram Swarup walked backwards, and took up a position standing against the wall a few paces from his wife.

Sitting Amanti at the central table also proved a problem. She regarded the chair with amused suspicion, and it occurred to Priestman that she had probably not sat in one before. She sat down fast. When it was apparent that the seat did not bite, she looked up at Priestman, and raised her eyebrows as though to say, 'now, what next?'

Priestman had little idea how to begin the lesson. He had dismissed as tedious a picture book of cows and horses with their Hindi names beneath. He had considerable confidence in his powers of playing it by ear.

'Table,' said Priestman tapping it jovially.

'Table,' repeated Amanti also tapping it and returning his smile.

'Um, er, chair,' said Priestman frowning slightly, and indicating the object.

'Um, er, chair,' repeated Amanti looking solemn.

'No, just chair.'

'No, just chair.'

'Ah,' said Priestman.

'Ah?'

He looked around trying to think of something else to point out.

'Book?' queried Amanti, indicating one with an air of helping him out.

'Yes. Book. Very good. You know some English? More, more.' He made encouraging gestures with his hands.

'Good morning, sir. Ball. Stupid boy. Clear off you little bastards.' Amanti watched Priestman carefully as he moved uneasily in his chair. He got up and started to walk about, alternately laughing to himself and frowning.

'Right,' he said stopping before her. 'Let's be practical.' He brought a vase, a cup, a pencil, and a rubber. He told her their names, then sat a little way off, and had her bring him the objects and take them back to the table. Then he had her bring him several objects at a time, and she learned to do it all remarkably quickly. Then he reversed their roles and had her ask him for the objects, and though this proved harder for her, and incredible to Ram Swarup who stood mouth agape at the sight of his daughter ordering the sahib about, she soon mastered it. And Priestman's earlier realization, that she had been gently making fun of him, changed to admiration and unease when she added the word 'please' in front of her requests, whereas he had omitted it. Her movements about the room were graceful and assured. She did not stoop when she walked, and when she sat, it was calmly and with none of the pulling of sari about the face or the downcast looks at the lap which characterized the movements of so many of the Indian women he had met. Then she sat close to him. And for the first time he caught the powerful, acrid smell of her. It brought to him a feeling of panic, followed swiftly by a sense of great comfort. He was puzzled at such an emotional reaction to a simple, definite but not unpleasant smell.

When she and her parents had left, he sat thinking over the lesson and preparing the next. He put the pencil into the cup and twirled it, saying aloud: 'What a really nice girl. What a pity.' Then he went to dinner.

After the meal, Panwar brought Priestman contributions for the fortnightly School Review. This would be the third issue that he had edited, his first having been a rushed number reporting Founder's Day.

'There are some items,' said Panwar looking worried, 'that I think you should look at first. They are not very nice.'

'Oh, good, some controversy at last!'

'It is more than that.' Panwar handed Priestman the sheets of paper. The first letter read:

Sir, I will not inform you of the weather or of recent politics, but come straight to the point. Several Old Boys have informed me that their names have been omitted from the list of first division exam passes published in the post Founder's Day number. I and many others would be glad if the editors paid more attention to facts of interest, and less to literary impressions about ephemera.

Yours etc, Cross.

'Oh. We've dropped a brick,' said Priestman laughing. 'Well, we can put it right.'

'Yes. But I cannot understand how the page with the omitted names went missing. Apart from that, his remarks about the weather and politics were references to the subject of your first editorial.'

'They weren't the subject. I simply mentioned them in passing. Anyway I don't expect everyone to like my leaders.'

'Yes. But it is too well written to come from a boy.'

'Never mind. We'll get the names and publish them with an apology. What's this next tale of woe?' Priestman read it aloud:

Sir, In recent issues we note with dismay that the English section of the Review has expanded to the detriment of the Hindi section. Was it for this that we won Independence over a quarter of a century ago?

Yours, Patriot.

'Oh dear. What am I supposed to do about that?'

'Nothing. It is nothing to do with you. There are never enough contributions to the Hindi section. It is not really contracting. The letter is just mischievous.'

'Alright. I'll put an editor's note under the letter saying that as soon as the editor has learned enough Hindi, he intends to contribute to the Hindi section himself.'

'Very good,' laughed Panwar. 'But that one you are holding is much more serious.'

Priestman read:

Sir, We have heard that some members of staff go on interesting cycle trips with friends. They make exciting explorations, and have all sorts of interesting experiences.

132

It has been a tradition of this school that staff take boys on cycle trips. While not wishing to criticize staff, it seems a pity that our ancient traditions should be so flagrantly cast aside.

'Yes, that's very slippery, and I shan't publish it.'

'You realize, Edward, that these letters form a concerted campaign to vilify you?'

'Oh, surely not?'

'You know that Arun Sen has now moved to his new quarters near the Junior School?'

'Oh well. But it can't be him behind all these letters, surely? He wouldn't want the Hindi section to expand. Anyway, I tried to interest him in helping with the Review and our other activities.'

'You know he was expecting to be made editor before you came.'

'And I suggested to the principal that he should be, but he insisted I should do it. Yes, I can see he must be angry with me. Well, I shall just have to beard the "King Lion" in his new lair. You know, the way he talked about Miss Willcox led me to believe that she had become an embarrassment to him. I thought he would be glad to see the back of her.'

'He is certainly well rid of her.'

'Well, I intend to see her again and the nurse as soon as I can. I may be able to help them in some way. I suppose a reference from me might possibly be helpful.'

'I think you should now forget them, Edward. The principal has given references. My father will do something. Forget them.'

'But you're a bad fellow to cry off from my lesson with the servant girl. No, it didn't matter. You know, if I can develop a sort of course with her, it will come in very useful when we get to grips with the problem of education in the villages.'

'You still cannot tell me about these plans?'

'I think I can tell you that it involves major schemes to modernize this state, and the Rani wishes me to take a large part in it. In fact I should have heard from her by now. But please don't say anything about it to anyone yet. Anyway, I know you're not the sort, like Mattacharya and Patel, to go running to the principal with every bit of gossip. Tell me, is Arun like that too?'

'No, no. It is only senior masters who are allowed to do that, and editors of the Review.' Panwar got up to leave.

'Do you want a torch? It's rather dark tonight.'

'No, thank you. I shall stamp my feet to keep snakes away.'

As Panwar passed the large water tank, he thought he heard the sound of gentle splashing coming from it. He knew that the boys would not dare to bathe in such dirty water. Anyway it was too dark to see. He hurried back to his room. It was lonely there now after the departure of Arun Sen. Once in bed, he took up the stage sword and twirled it vaguely. In one corner of the room stood a green and gold lance with a silver painted point. He put down the sword, and took from beneath his pillow a photograph of the cast of *Macbeth* taken the day after the play. Some boys wore their costumes; others wore their blazers which bore on the pocket the school crest, a cannon with battlement at its tail, and beneath the motto: 'Fortitude not Aggression'. He examined the photograph intently for several minutes before replacing it. He got up and turned off the light at the switch near the door. Taking up the spear, he stood for a while at the open door before returning to bed.

19

His Highness the Rajah of Karatpore reclined on his couch-like throne in the marble durbar hall of the palace. He observed the court seated cross-legged in two rows down the room. His long white coat almost concealed his white trousers, tight at the ankles. His turban resembled an ocean-going canoe; high at prow and stern, it seemed from the front to be cresting the wave of his head, and to be about to journey on. The moustache, which had waxed so high when about to greet the Maharajah, now fell thick to his chin. The eyelids, formerly raised in startled greeting, now drooped as one by one his courtiers came forward to pay homage. For some of them, such as his relative Major Rao, the commander-in-chief, his eyes lit up and he rocked to and fro. To those who displeased him, he closed his eyes completely. The principal was among those thus unfavoured. To those he despised, he turned his head away as well; Banglaratnam was among the despised. The Rajah reflected that in former days such a man as Banglaratnam would not have been present. But the numbers of his court were now depleted. The Rajah also remembered how whenever there was trouble at the school the principal pleaded for Banglaratnam to be present. The Rajah reflected upon the glories of his father's durbars before the war, remembered the faces now long gone, and considered what would be left to pass on to his son. Economies must be made, but his position maintained. Now he felt his position threatened still further for he held in his left hand the memorandum from Priestman to the Rani, and the letter from the 'Viceroy' to the dowager Rani.

When the homage of all had been paid, there was silence as they awaited the Rajah's speech. Banglaratnam, the only one not in Indian dress, looked serious and startled by turns. He cleared his throat and the principal frowned at him. Then the

135

slight rustle of the peacock-feather fans above the Rajah's head could be heard, together with the attenuated cries of crows in the afternoon sunlight outside, and the faint *chug-chug* of the generator needed to power the many lights of the central chandelier, though it was quite light enough without them. The sour smell of diesel oil mingled with the clean, soapy scent of incense. The Rajah sniffed at his wrist. Perhaps even the expensive scent he used would have to go.

Then he quietly began his speech, touching first upon general matters of state which held nothing new for the audience, then on the security of the state. Gradually his voice became more firm, then shrill as he came to particulars.

'And it has been brought to our notice that not only are we threatened in a general way by those who have always wished us harm, and who daily interfere with us on our doorstep, but that now foreign spies are employed in our midst in the disguise of educationalists and reformers. They spread rumours that we have perpetrated famine and persecution.' There was a stir of disquiet among the audience. The Rajah's voice rose still higher.

'They would carry such rumours even to the ears of those who by blood should be our friends, but who now wax proud and fat, traitors in the enemy camp.' He waved the pieces of paper, and shouted. 'I tell you there is poison in our cups!' The audience murmured louder in real alarm. Those who did not know what the Rajah's outburst was about glared at Banglaratnam, and the principal too turned and glared at him.

After the speech, there was much angry talk as betel nut and scent were distributed, and lime juice poured into metal cups. Banglaratnam dropped his. There was a sudden silence. The cup rolled a few paces, and a courtier pushed it away angrily with his foot.

Then the principal and Banglaratnam were summoned to a private audience chamber where the Rajah, his prime minister and the commander-in-chief, Major Rao, stood looking fierce.

'Failed again,' said the Rajah to the principal quietly. 'Why will you not stay on your elephant patch? Why will you not get a proper Englishman? That Macgregor fellow was not enough for you. Now we have your new chap roaming around the countryside with maps, saying your village of Bhonsa is responsible for killing people. Why is this fellow Priestman allowed to roam without an escort?'

'I gave specific instructions,' said the principal glaring at Banglaratnam.

'I just turned my back and he was gone,' said Banglaratnam. 'But government reports show there is no famine.'

'So they say to us,' said the Rajah. 'But what have they reported elsewhere, I ask myself?'

'Aha,' agreed Major Rao knowingly.

'If only you had got the right sort of Englishman,' sighed the Rajah, 'my darling princeling would not have had to go to England, would not have been lost to us in the mist. What is the good of having my own English school, if my own child cannot go to it? Now we hear he has the most heavy cold. Her Highness is absolutely distracted beyond belief.' There was a general murmur of distress.

'At Throgton School he would have been so well looked after,' sighed Banglaratnam.

'Throgton, Frogtown? What is this place?' snapped the Rajah. 'My son goes to a proper English school.'

'It may be,' said the tall ascetic-looking prime minister, 'that Mr Priestman is lonely. I hear that he has not been too well for some time, and that there is no longer a nurse at the school clinic.'

'Is this so?' queried the Rajah of the principal.

'It is so, your Highness,' said the principal. 'I try myself very hard to amuse him.'

'Yes,' said Banglaratnam, 'I am amusing him constantly all the time without cease.'

'Ha! That accounts for it!' barked Major Rao.

'He is, after all, our guest,' said the prime minister gently.

'How true,' said the Rajah. 'You always remind me of what is right.' He became agitated, and started to pace the room, one hand on the prow of his turban. 'This is terrible, terrible. We have a guest. He is sick. He receives no medical attention, and is driven mad by some fellow from the south trying to amuse him.'

'The principal also amuses him,' retorted Banglaratnam.

'I hardly see him,' exclaimed the principal hotly. 'He is being deliberately kept from me.'

'That is enough!' snapped the Rajah. 'We must think of a plan.'

'Definitely we must have a plan,' echoed Banglaratnam.

For a while they deliberated. It was agreed that Priestman should be feted in January after the holidays. He would be invited to the palace.

'But we must do something for him now as well,' said the Rajah. 'Soon he goes to the Maharajah. That fellow will pump him about us. He must carry good reports. We must do something for him that he will really like.'

'He wanted to fly with you, your Highness, very much,' said the principal smiling. 'It is only big planes he dislikes.'

'He wanted to fly with me?' cried the Rajah. 'Why was I not told of this? This is marvellous. Of course he must fly. When will the plane be ready?'

'By Tuesday we will have lift off again,' said Major Rao.

'Then on Tuesday he will fly with me. How happy I am!' They all beamed.

'But,' added Major Rao, 'there must be no more trouble, no more interference, or there will be one hell of a row. Dismissals, eh what?'

'Hangings!' cried the Rajah jovially. 'Major Rao will kick up one hell of a row for you school fellows.' He slapped the major on the back.

'I suppose,' said the prime minister, 'that Mr Priestman will be here in August for Gokul Astami festival, and see Lord Krishna born.'

'Ah, he will be here,' said the principal.

The Rajah's face took on the expression of devotion.

'Ah, he will see the Lord of Creation born,' echoed Major Rao, and his fierce little eyes became gentle and clouded with tears.

'How I long to meet Mr Priestman,' sighed the Rajah. 'He must be such a beautiful soul. So many varied interests. You must sound him out. Perhaps he would be my private secretary. An English private secretary just as my poor dear father had.' His face became distressed, and the others took on a look of anguish. 'And tutor to our darling, our beloved princeling lost to us in the mists of an alien land.'

138

20

The evening was cold, and there was no moon when Priestman set out on the mile-long walk to Arun Sen's new quarters. He had changed into heavy boots for the walk, and he stamped them to scare snakes from the path. For the first time in India he wore his suede fur-lined top coat. He felt pleasantly cool and wide awake. The night was scented, and the sounds of record players came from the boys' common rooms. He called out to the night watchman at the entrance to the Senior School. The man thrust his stick beneath his left arm, and coming to attention, barked out an efficient, 'night, sahib!', and went off stamping and banging his arms to keep warm.

It was much darker on the road between the two schools, and Priestman wished he had brought his torch. A hiss came from in front of him. He waited while a long and thick python leisurely made its way across the road.

He continued, sensing rather than seeing the shape of the temple to his left where *Macbeth* had been staged. There were only a few lights still shining in the Junior School because its boys went to bed earlier. Before him loomed a greater patch of darkness where the ruins of the fortress of Sena Suj stood beside the Monkey Gate. On his right was a cluster of single-storey buildings.

Priestman was not sure which was Arun Sen's. He approached, and called his name. A boy of about twelve came out of the darkness and raised a lamp to identify the visitor.

'Arun Sen Sahib?' enquired Priestman. The boy smiled and beckoned him to follow.

Arun Sen stood in the middle of the room. He greeted Priestman politely but with reserve, and kept him standing while he gave instructions to the boy, who disappeared into a room at the back. Though the main room was low, it was of a comfortable size, square, and altogether, thought Priestman, a considerable improvement on the passage-like place and cupboard he had shared with Panwar. There were rugs on the walls, a carpet on the floor, and bright cushions on two low divans. Everything was clean and neat, but the smell of sweet incense overpowering.

'Please, please, sit down,' exclaimed Arun as though Priestman were standing on too much ceremony. Priestman smiled, reflecting that in the earlier days of their acquaintance, he would have simply flung himself on to the nearest chair or Panwar's bed without thinking twice. 'I have asked tea to be brought. I hope that is alright. It is preferable to the appalling coffee we have.'

'Fine. Well, I can certainly see why you moved. You've done it up very well.'

'One could get no work done in the other place.' He indicated a pile of books on the central oval table. 'I am at last able to make the contribution to the Review you are always asking me for.'

'That is good news. What's it about?'

'Man-eating lions in Africa. The boys are always interested in these things.'

The servant boy came and pleasantly served the tea while Arun spoke to him gently, all the time giving him instructions by example which the boy carried out well and with evident pleasure.

'Who is your servant?' asked Priestman.

'He is a boy from my village. I sent for him to train him. His family has served mine for generations. He is deaf, poor boy. But he is very willing and careful.' Arun smiled at the boy, and indicated that he could leave. And Priestman too smiled at the pleasant child as he left.

'I'm sorry you've moved so far away, Arun. I had hoped we would see more of each other, and work together more.'

'You are angry with me?' Arun Sen laughed, and toyed with a vase on the table, picking it up and replacing it in different positions.

'Of course not. I just thought you might have wanted to become more of the team, share the load a bit.'

'Yes. You are angry with me. This is terrible.' His eyes darted around the room, and he went to rearrange some cushions on the other divan.

'I don't get angry with people,' said Priestman. He sat perched on the edge of the divan. It semed to him rude even to unbutton his coat. 'You don't have to help us. You do your regular work very well. I know that the societies, plays and things can be a bore. I don't blame you. Anyway, you and I haven't exactly hit it off. I've not been too helpful to you.'

'Not hit it off? Not helpful? How can you say this?'

'Miss Willcox? That was hardly helpful. It's you who should be angry with me.'

Arun picked up a chair and sat down facing Priestman. He leant forward and tapped Priestman on the knee. 'I am grateful. She had become insatiable. Indiscreet. Her departure was a godsend.'

'Well, I'm glad for you, then. But sorry for her. You should have come on the trip, then nothing would have happened.'

'Something more jolly might have happened.' He cocked his head and winked at Priestman.

'So. We're not enemies?' Priestman looked at the floor.

'What a dreadful thought! I have always been your friend. But – and you must forgive me – you are so very British, Edward. I am sometimes scared of you.' He laughed, and looked unscared.

'It's just the not-so-great British reserve. It doesn't mean anything. It's the way one was brought up. Did you know I was brought up to rule an empire? No, really. You know that educational methods are slow to catch up with political realities. Look at this school.'

'Yes. But I think you are romanticizing a little, Edward.'

'Possibly, but not much. You know about my family's connections with India. And a general came to my prep school once. He was braided, very impressive and flushed from a good lunch with the headmaster. "Soon," he cried sternly, "you will be scattered to the four corners of the empire. You are its future leaders!" Ten years later I went to the careers master and said: "To which corner am I to be scattered, sir?" And he said: "Too late. The empire was finally lost last year. But I've got this job making washing-machines in Slough." So I went to university

141

instead. And afterwards at the university appointments bureau they had this appointment marketing washing-machine modules out of Slough. So I went on the grand tour instead – Europe, now here.

'But why here, Edward? This is such a dismal place. It is just a poor copy of the good schools in India. There is a really good school not a hundred miles from here whose chief guests have included Mountbatten and Nehru. None of us could get a job there. Really you are wasting your time in this place.'

'And you?'

'I cannot be so choosey. Besides it suits me, particularly now. I make no secret of my strong leaning towards the ladies.' He looked around his room and smiled with satisfaction. 'But you have said nothing to me of love, Edward. For you, from the liberated West, this place must be an emotional desert.'

'The love of my life did not love me so I fled to your desert. No, I'm not entirely joking. Last night I wrote her a never-to-be posted farewell. Here, read it for yourself.'

Arun read the letter while Priestman frowned with embarrassment. When he had finished, Arun gave him back the paper. 'Really, Edward, this was a great love. I cannot understand why it was not requited. The letter is very beautiful.'

'Now it seems to me strained. The ravings of the small hours. Better destroyed. But I just wanted to show you I was human. I haven't shown that sort of thing to anyone else before. I don't suppose I will again.'

'Really, Edward, I am very moved. It was a very Indian gesture. You are quite like one of us. And you are so popular with the boys.'

'A shaky basis. But the honeymoon is over. Rebellion is in the air. One class, for example, don't want to read *Hamlet* and say so, because it's not on the syllabus.'

'You must explain and be firm. Or you should drop it straight away. Perhaps that would be best. And Edward, since you have been so open with me, may I suggest something? Drop all this business of your missing village. People are beginning to talk. Of course your concern does you great credit, but. . .'

'They think I'm cracked in the head.'

'Of course not.'

'Next week I go with the Rajah in his plane. If we can't find it, that's the end of the matter.'

'This is marvellous news. You will surely find it if it is there.'

'Yes.'

There was a pause in the conversation. Priestman felt he had better go.

'Well, I must be off.' Arun Sen smiled and did not try to dissuade him. Priestman went over to the table, and looked at the papers. 'So, when may we expect the great work?'

'It is getting so long.' Arun smiled and gathered the papers together.

'We could serialize it.'

'You are too kind.'

'No, really. You were so good helping with the first number I had to edit. Why don't you help us still?'

'You see, I do not like to say this,' Arun moistened his lips and continued, 'but Panwar and I have fallen out a little. It would be difficult. He thinks I do not want to live with him. It is silly. We just had no privacy.'

'Oh dear. So complicated.'

'Shall I get my boy to light your way back?'

'No thanks. But I wouldn't mind a torch. I saw an enormous python on the road near the temple.'

'A real python?'

'Yes. You know I'm not given to seeing things which don't exist all the time. And when I do see paper snakes, I know they are paper snakes – eventually, anyway.'

They both laughed, and Priestman went back somewhat relieved and pleased with the outcome of his visit.

As he neared his quarters, he heard a noise from the direction of the cannon. He went to investigate. He could just make out three figures. There were two boys and a girl. The girl was astride the cannon. He thought it was Amanti, with Ashok and his servant friend. But they saw him approaching, and made off fast. He ran his hands over the cannon. He regretted that he had disturbed them. It was not his business if Ashok was out late. Patel should take care of that. They were happy, and he admired all three of them. For the first time he began to feel lonely in this place. He regretted that Amanti could not laugh and talk naturally with him. He felt the letter in his pocket. Two years now since they had said goodbye, though they had hardly said that; just not seen one another. He crumpled the letter and went to the battlements intending to throw it over them. He looked out over the palace to the direction of Bhonsa. And that single light which bobbed, disappeared, then reappeared – well, it could be anything. Would it ever stop, he wondered, this nagging need to improve himself, improve the world? No matter how he tried to ignore it, he knew that there was only one thing that mattered to him – by his efforts to leave the world a better place than when he had come into it. And it was now, in this place that the opportunity which had so unexpectedly presented itself had to be seized. 'Past, past,' he murmured as he went forward, and tearing the letter into scraps, threw them over the edge; and the sounds of the town which welled up to him seemed to reply: 'Here. Now.'

21

For her next lesson, Amanti came with only her mother who sat outside on the terrace. Ram Swarup was away at Bhonsa forwarding the marriage negotiations. They sat at the table going through a little book of world geography he had borrowed from Patel. Then Priestman decided that since they were now free from constant observation, he would have Amanti move around even more. 'Amanti, please bring me some water.'

'Where is water?'

'The water is in the bathroom.' She had to pass through his bedroom to get the water. She hesitated. 'Go on. Take a cup from the little table, and bring me some water in the cup, please.'

Cautiously she entered the dark bedroom, then slipped quickly through to the lighter, more airy bathroom. After a moment he followed her. She was gazing at the strange objects: the basin, lavatory and bath.

'What is that?' she asked, pointing at the bath.

'That is a bath.' He put in the plug, ran some water, and mimed the actions of undressing and getting into the bath. She smiled understanding.

'What is that?' she enquired, pointing at the lavatory. He threw some toilet paper into it.

'This is a chain. Pull the chain.' She did so and stood back in astonishment at the gush and swirl of water.

After the tap water had been brought to him in the other room, Priestman had Amanti give him the orders. Then they had fun giving each other orders to stop, go, turn left and right, Priestman falling over chairs or marching into the wall when she did not call 'stop' in time. Then they found themselves together in the bedroom.

'This is my bed. And this is a mosquito net. Buzz, buzz.' She leant forward and cautiously felt the netting. The action disturbed a large mosquito trapped inside the net.

'Do you like buzz buzz in bed?' queried Amanti frowning.

'Mosquitoes? No!' said Priestman pulling a face. 'Mosquitoes should be outside.' She laughed and he reached under the net and tried to kill the mosquito.

'No, no!' cried Amanti, and pushing past him she waited till the insect had settled, then cupped it in her hands. 'Good mosquito.' She frowned, struggling to express herself.

'I understand. Bad Edward Sahib.'

'Not bad Edward Sahib.'

'Edward Sahib must learn to be kind to little things.' He put forward a hand and stroked above her cupped hands. 'I will learn from you, Amanti.'

Her mother's voice came from the verandah door. Amanti brushed past him. She turned at the door, 'I must go now, Edward Sahib.' The mother spoke again.

'See you tomorrow.'

She nodded and left, her hands still cupped around the insect.

When the appointed time came for her next lesson, she did not arrive. Priestman called for Ram Swarup, and had a boy translate for him. It appeared that Amanti had had enough lessons.

'He is asking for some paper,' said the boy.

'Tell him I will give him his paper but not yet. He can go.'

Ram Swarup understood the anger in Priestman's voice, and left. Once alone Priestman was at a loss what to do with himself. He now realized that he had been looking forward to the lesson more than he had thought possible. He had made plans for it. He had made out a rough course of lessons for her. Instead of simply learning the language, she would gain knowledge. He had planned to show her photographs of his home and family, to start arithmetic and biology. The child had proved so quick to learn, so amused and amusing that what had once been a duty, he now realized had become a delight. If necessary he would withhold the certificate from Ram Swarup. After five minutes of these frustrated deliberations, he went to see Panwar to whom he complained bitterly.

'She was getting on so well. And now her father wants his idiotic paper.'

'That was all he ever wanted.'

'It's monstrous.'

'Edward, you like the child don't you? You find her very sweet, and you are a dedicated teacher.'

'Hm. I know you think I should leave it. But don't you see how false it is if we pay lip service to the idea of education, then only give it to those whose parents can pay?'

'I agree. I hate all these fat businessmen parents.'

'You don't like it here really, do you?'

'I too am working for my piece of paper. Besides where else would I get the chance of working under a real Englishman?'

'You don't work under me. Anyway, your reference will be earned. But I'm not going to let this matter rest.'

'Edward, once I did not prevent you from doing something – the cycle trip – when I should have warned you much more strongly against it.'

'I see. I'm supposed to be on the verge of making another great mistake. Well I really can't see why.'

'There has been some silly talk that you are more interested in educating the Harijan girl than the boys.'

'I bitterly resent that. I give a few lessons to one scorned and deprived child, and the whole bloody place is up in arms.'

'No, no. It is just some silly talk by some people.'

'It always is.' Priestman stood up and started to move about the room, picking up the spear and then the stage sword. It gave him some satisfaction to grip it tightly. 'Please do this one thing for me. See the girl and the father together with me. Find out if I've done anything to offend them.'

'How could you offend them?'

'Oh I don't know. My scheme of practical teaching involved the child going to get things from my bathroom and bedroom. Everybody in this country seems to have potential sexual outrage on the brain. Perhaps that has offended them.'

'It would be better if you dropped all this. Please don't be angry. Nothing is private here. Anyway, it is possible some of the

147

higher caste servants are resenting these lessons. They would make it hard for your servant. That is probably happening. To push him too hard would not be good for his position.'

Priestman sighed, and was silent for a while. He ruffled through some of the exercise books lying on Panwar's bed. He put down the sword, and Panwar quietly replaced it beside his bed.

'You mark very thoroughly, Panwar. Your family are all teachers aren't they? It makes a difference.'

'And your parents?'

'Manufacturing. My father wasn't bright enough for the Indian Civil Service, and the army didn't appeal to him. I shouldn't knock engineering. It gave me my expensive education. Perhaps one should do what one's parents did. Look, you must always tell me if I'm going wrong.'

'It must be very lonely here for you in such a strange country without your own people.'

'Oh, I don't really miss them. But I do miss silly things. How basic this country makes one. I miss red wine, for example, and a certain type of food I am not allowed to mention to you.'

'English cows are not holy cows,' said Panwar laughing.

'Thank God for that! Well, I'll leave you to your marking.'

22

For the remaining few days before the plane trip with the Rajah, Priestman found himself frequently stationed behind the wire netting of the verandah doors. He waited eagerly for the women to come in the evening and fill their pots and cans at the tap. But Amanti, once a frequent visitor, came less often, and quickly left.

During his first few days at the school, he had sat on the verandah watching the women and the sunset beyond. But soon the attacks of insects, and the ever-present possibility of snakes had made him give up the verandah. Moreover, his Indian guests had no desire to sit out there. Now, to sit there openly seemed to him out of the question since it would constitute an infringement of the women's privacy. He reflected ruefully on the frivolous plans he had made that first day for a garden and a bar.

When the women had finished drawing water, he would often go for a walk in the gathering dusk to the cannon, and place his hand upon it, remembering how Amanti had sat astride it. During these walks he began to work out in more detail his plans for the school and the state. Things would be different when he had power. Should he accept the position of principal, or make sure that somebody had it who would make the changes he considered necessary? Panwar was too junior and too timid for such a post. None of the other members of staff was suitable. No, the best idea would be to have somebody young and energetic from England who would think like him. But in order to carry out his future work in this state, he felt that he needed a partner who was thoroughly of the people. Modernization must not be an imposition from outside. More frequently in his walks around the fort, he conducted conversations in his mind with Amanti whom he imagined walking beside him. They spoke freely together in friendship and shared endeavour. In his mind, she was several years older. She gave him information in detail about village life, cutting through the tangled webs of caste, family relationships, and social organization generally, and pointing the way forward or confirming his own ideas about the solutions to specific problems. They had developed shared jokes, the intimacy of silence, mock arguments.

He became increasingly irritated by what he considered the trivial social barriers that surrounded Indian women. His irritation began to show itself in pointed remarks to members of staff, in a readiness to bring up the subject of the erotic statues of Khajuraho where, it was said 'one is embarrassed to take one's children'.

Matters came to a head on a Saturday evening before the plane trip, when he curtly ordered Ram Swarup to take a note to the housemaster, Patel. Priestman was alone and the idea of Saturday night with no entertainment got on his nerves. The note read: 'Dear Mr Patel, have you got any drink around the place, whisky or even beer? I'll pay you for it.'

Ram Swarup returned with the note, and explained sorrowfully that he had been unable to deliver it and that Patel had chased him away.

Priestman shouted 'bloody hell' and rushed next door. Banging loudly on the open door, he went in to greet the surprised Patel. As he entered the room, Patel's wife and another woman jumped up and went behind a curtain.

'Good evening, Mrs Patel,' said Priestman in a cold, loud voice at her retreating back. He turned to Patel. 'Doesn't your wife care to acknowledge me? I suppose I have done something to offend her. And I suppose I've offended you as well, since you won't acknowledge my servant and the message he brought.'

'Please, please. There is no offence. Sit down, please.'

'No. It's alright thank you. I'm not staying. My servant is a human being and is waiting for me. I don't like to keep him waiting.'

'Please forgive my wife. She is very old-fashioned.'

'Purdah, you mean.'

'It is a silly custom, but it is so difficult to get women to change.

150

Your servant – any other time I would have been glad to accept your written message from him, but that other lady is my sister-in-law who is visiting us. If she saw me taking a message from an untouchable, it would be reported at their home. My wife's family would be very angry.'

'Well I am very angry. I know that's not so important. But I'm not angry for myself but for my servant who, to mention just one thing you may understand, is distressed that he has been unable to carry out my commission.'

'What was the commission? Tell me and I will carry it out myself.'

'Oh, nothing. Well, well, there it is. But I thought this sort of treatment was against the law.'

'Mr Priestman, I beg you to understand. A few years ago if an untouchable's shadow fell across me I would be forced to perform lengthy ablutions. That is finished now. We are moving forward.'

'Yes, yes. So I see. Goodnight.' As he was leaving, Patel rushed out after him.

'Mr Priestman. Come to dinner next week. My wife is an excellent cook. She will serve us and then she will come and talk with us. She is an informed and intelligent lady. Really she would like to meet you.' Patel put out his hand and took Priestman by the arm and looked sorrowfully at him. 'You are unhappy about something else too. It is lonely for you here. The principal feels it badly. He worries so. We all worry that you are alone without your own people.'

Priestman let out a long sigh. 'How untouchable am I?' he asked.

'No, no, no!' cried Patel in distress.

'In that case, forgive my rudeness and my anger, but not their cause.' Priestman briefly embraced Patel and hurried away, adding that he would be glad to come to dinner.

It had become increasingly cold over the last few days. There were reports that many of the homeless who slept in the streets of the town below had died of cold. Fifteen bodies had been discovered that morning in the central square. The boys said that a thin film of ice had covered the water tank, though it had melted by the time Priestman had passed it on his way to school.

Now Priestman realized as he regained his rooms that the fort was shrouded in dense mist. He too felt the cold, and decided that all that was left for him now was to go to bed. He considered that tomorrow he would go to breakfast unshaven, then retire again to bed till lunch. His beard he would explain as being in honour of the anniversary of his great grandmother's birth, when his caste forbade him to shave, or to be spoken to for the rest of the day.

As he lay in bed considering elaborations of this theme which might come in useful and at least would amuse him, he heard a slight noise from the living room. He seized the hockey stick with pleasure, hoping that he would discover an enormous cobra and that he would kill it after quite a fight. Entering the living room, he heard the noise again; somebody was trying the verandah door. No school boy ever entered that way, and he had told Ram Swarup more than an hour ago to go to bed. So it was a thief after his carelessly hidden money, and a thief would be a more amusing adversary than a snake. Yes, thieves would be out in such a mist.

He crept to the door and listened, stick raised. Then he heard her voice, whispering, 'Edward Sahib, Amanti.' He opened the door slightly, and she slipped quickly under his arm.

'Amanti,' he whispered closing the door quietly, 'you should not have come.' He went to turn on the lights, but she was standing in front of the switch. She waved her hand back and forth across her body and pointed to the bedroom. It was true that in the bedroom they would be safe from prying eyes. By contrast, the living room doors were cracked in places particularly on the verandah side where there was direct sun for most of the day.

Amanti seemed to have taken charge. She carried her usual chair from the living room into the bedroom. Then she fetched the book of world geography, and adjusted the shade of the bedside lamp so that it gave more light. The book she put on the bed.

'Your mother and father will be angry, Amanti. You must go soon.' He seated himself on the bed.

'Mother and father. . .' She put her hand under her head to indicate that they were asleep. 'Amanti is little mouse.' She

152

narrowed her eyes, and moved her fingers up and down to illustrate tip-toeing. 'Many times, Amanti is little mouse at night. Little room too hot. No moon. I swim in tank. No sari, blanket. Like boy at night.' She seemed to be wearing only a shift beneath her blanket. She was very pleased with her deception. 'But tonight too cold. No swim.'

'But people will think bad things about you – and about me.'

'I not bad girl. You not bad man. You not Macgregor Sahib.'

'Hurrah, at last somebody realizes I am not Macgregor!'

'I learn. You teach. Good.' She tapped the book.

He started to explain the pictures, but it was difficult to make her understand where they were. So he turned to the map of the world, and linked England with India by recounting his air journey and the time it took to cover the distance. The distance from Delhi to Karatpore he explained in train time and then in walking time. All this involved calculations on paper so that he was able to impart some elementary mathematics. And all the time he was able to take in the details of her earnest profile and watch the movement of her finely boned hands as she turned a page or held a finger on a particular picture. It was only occasionally that he caught from her the strange smell he had noticed on the first day. Now he found himself trying to catch that faint odour, and when he did it was very pleasant to him.

Sometimes the blanket fell slightly from her knees, and he noticed with pleasure the absent-minded way in which she replaced it, so unlike the practised plucking at their saris of the older women. Only her youth now came to him as a surprise, so often had he thought of her as almost adult. Yet that adjustment to the threadbare blanket carried more charm for him than all the twirling of models in a salon or the studied movements of European women on a Mediterranean beach. And he realized that the naturalness of her movements were akin to those of his former love and that the two women were of a kind. They both had humour, intelligence, kindness and a physical beauty which they discounted almost as an inconvenience.

As she pored over the book, and looked at him earnestly for information, it came to him with regret that were she able to continue her education fully, she would in all probability outstrip him; that she had a quickness and independence of mind –

153

qualities which he had only partly been able to acquire, and that he had lost the capacity for delight. Though part of his mind told him that any further relationship between them was not possible, and that any attempt at such a relationship could only bring harm to them both, he still wondered whether, if he were bold enough, there was not some way in which they could break out into that new shared life he had so vividly imagined. But instead they spoke now in whispers and each moment was charged with the possibility of discovery.

The falseness of their present situation brought back to him the irritation he had felt so strongly earlier in the evening. He looked at his watch which said half-past one. Her eyes were sleepy and happy as she crept with him to the door, on tip-toe like a mouse, in mock fear.

'So when will you come again? When you come here for lesson?' Now he thought, she is in charge, and since she seems so at home in the night, let her choose. She counted off three fingers on her hand. 'Tuesday? In the day I go flying with the Rajah.' He made his meaning clear by signs. 'But at night you come.' As he opened the door, he showed her how he would leave it unlocked for her, and she understood and agreed.

23

After breakfast on Tuesday, Priestman's packed lunch was brought to him, and he waited to be collected and driven to the palace. He wore a tough bush jacket and shorts. When the Rajah's A.D.C. arrived in a jeep, Priestman asked the pleasant young man whether or not his dress was suitable. The A.D.C. suggested that long trousers would be more suitable, so Priestman changed.

The A.D.C. drove the four miles to the palace rather recklessly. He talked all the time about the latest cars and aircraft, and how he hoped to go with the Rajah next year to Europe and visit the motor and air shows.

They drove to a large stable in the palace grounds. It had been converted and additions made to form a hangar. They were met by a very gentlemanly head groom to the Rajah. This man, who spoke good English, showed Priestman several beautifully polished aircraft which were evidently his pride, but which were no longer airworthy because of lack of spare parts.

The A.D.C. returned to say that they were ready to move off. They walked round to the front of the palace where a four-wheel-drive vehicle stood. Here Priestman was introduced to the Rajah's cousin or uncle, it was hard to ascertain which. He was a short, stout, military-looking man. He spoke very fast with a sort of Sandhurst accent difficult to follow.

When Priestman asked how far it was to the Rajah's plane, the relative looked puzzled, and explained that the Rajah had flown in it that morning to Bombay, and was not expected back for several days.

'We are going to see how many tiger are about,' said the relative. 'A real big shot comes next week, and he must shoot a tiger, ha, ha. It is the tradition. We will have to peg one out from the zoo if necessary, they are so scarce.'

'Illegal?' queried Priestman.

'Oh terribly illegal. Bah! Government. Hell.' The relative took the wheel. He drove at breakneck speed through the town, one hand pressing down the horn, scattering the people. 'These people hate us!' he shouted. 'They want me to run over one of them so they can make a fuss.'

The noise of the horn and the rushing wind in the open vehicle made it difficult to talk. When they reached more open country, Priestman asked: 'Are we going in the direction of Bhonsa?' He assumed that since the flight had been cancelled or postponed, they were at least going to take in the area around Bhonsa in order to search for the missing village. His question caused some confusion since it appeared that they had not heard of Bhonsa. When Priestman explained the village's relationship to the school, they understood. Priestman had simply mispronounced the name.

'No,' said the A.D.C. 'We are going in quite the opposite direction.'

'So,' thought Priestman, 'is this a misunderstanding, a deliberate mistake, a warning to me to forget the place, or just a distraction since I expressed interest to the principal in going on a hunting expedition? Whatever the explanation, it's just as well that we're not trying to find the village with this madman, who keeps ranting at the "damn natives". He would probably want to shoot the inhabitants.' Priestman began to wonder how he would get through the day. The groom was hanging on precariously to the tailboard, and the A.D.C. was jogging up and down in the back.

Several times Major Rao, for so he was called by the A.D.C., braked hard, and seizing a shotgun, leapt from the vehicle. He would then pursue small grey birds a few yards into the thorn bushes, and shoot at them as they ran. Even though he did not bag any, this unsportsman-like behaviour made Priestman dislike the man even more.

They came to a village surrounded by a thorn fence. A villager came out and spoke to the major, who told Priestman that a cow had been killed by a tiger ten days ago, but that no more activity

156

from tigers had since been reported.

The party made off through thick thorn scrub, so thick that the vehicle had to nose its way forward. They were silent because of the slowness and effort of their progress. The vehicle plunged and rolled. For a while Priestman enjoyed the adventure, which seemed to promise the sight of a tiger at any moment. He was pleased at the way his bush jacket withstood the thorns much better than the thin shirts of his companions.

After half an hour of this progress, they came to a clearing where there was a watch-tower beside the edge of a ravine. The ravine had steep banks, was green and deeply wooded. A stream ran through it. The A.D.C. remarked to Priestman that it was a very beautiful place. The man seemed to have a sweet nature, and Priestman readily agreed with him. On the opposite side of the ravine was a troop of monkeys. The groom kept pointing out separate groups of them to Priestman, and said that their presence high on the cliff indicated there were tigers in the ravine.

They entered the watch-tower or hide. It had two floors and slits in the walls for viewing out and shooting through.

'From here,' said Major Rao, 'I've seen them mating no farther than you are from me now, and shot them.'

'Ah,' replied Priestman trying to sound impressed. They waited for twenty minutes, Priestman hoping that they would see no tigers from that cowardly concrete emplacement. The thought of Amanti and of their meeting that evening dominated his thoughts.

When no animals came, they climbed out of the hide and had their lunch – for the most part in silence. Then they set off home. An uneventful journey. Once again the major stopped to shoot the little grey birds running over the hard rocky ground. This time he shot a brace.

As they drove up to the palace, a tall, ascetic man came forward. When the major saw him, his eyes lit up with a wonderful expression of pleasure. The stranger seemed equally pleased to see him. They made a strange contrast. And Priestman reflected how these people had raised friendship to a level he did not wish to attain. They had bonds of kinship, position, shared childhood. The intelligent man understood the silly man, and the latter was grateful. Priestman regretted how, by contrast, he was always critical of people, watching them, thinking to himself that such a person suited him while another did not.

'Prime Minister,' cried the major taking his hand, 'you are safe at last back among us. Five days! I have so much to tell you.'

'I hear already you have had so much trouble with the aeroplane. Will it ever fly?'

'Oh you have no idea the trouble. His Highness is in such a panic, poor man. And the wrong parts came. We tried to make them fit. And Pradeep smashed his hand so badly.'

They walked away hand in hand. There had been no intended rudeness to Priestman. They had simply forgotten his existence.

So was this to be the end of his search for the lost village – a search for a tiger which may have been there? He reflected that the intervention of others had proved only a hindrance, and that one had to rely on oneself. Yet the Rani had proved to be an area of sanity. He asked the A.D.C. if she was at home, but was told that she had gone with the Rajah.

'Where?' asked Priestman, knowing that the question was now impolite, but unable to stop himself. The A.D.C. smiled beautifully and said nothing.

Priestman asked the aide to drop him off in the town.

For a while he wandered about trying to find the crossroads where he had seen the little girl under the tree and the burst water pipe. But he became lost, and irritably hailed a taxi. He told the Sikh driver to take him to the best hotel in town.

There, Priestman sat in a small low-ceilinged room which was very brightly lit, and had plastic-topped tables like those in a cheap café. The place was not licensed to sell alcohol. He ordered some coffee. From where he sat, he could see the reception desk and beside it a room door numbered '201'. At another table sat a group of modern-looking young men, each of whom held or displayed from his tee-shirt pocket a packet of expensive international cigarettes.

Priestman left, and found the same taxi outside. He asked the driver to take him to the next best hotel in town.

Near the station, Priestman entered a large Victorian building called the Great Western Hotel. The spacious hall was pillared, and contained potted palms. At the base of the columns were the usual red stains of spat-out betel juice. Priestman went into a large dim room whose shutters were drawn against the late afternoon sun. He sat down on a stool at a long wooden counter. The rows of shelves behind the bar were empty. Behind the shelves was a large mirror etched with the flowing outline of a swan, and of a scantily clad woman. Her legs were together and her arms outstretched above her head which was bent far back so that she gazed at the ceiling. On one side of the mirror hung a cardboard advertisement for 'Gold Flake' cigarettes. On the other side, a Hollywood bathing belle embraced a bottle of cola as large as herself.

'Bang the counter and cry "shop", or the bugger won't come,' called a voice from the back of the room.

Priestman turned and saw three men sitting at a wicker table in a gloomy corner. 'Thanks,' he said. 'Shop!'

An old waiter appeared. He wore a cummerbund and turban.

'A pint of beer please,' said Priestman.

'I'm terribly sorry, sir,' said the waiter. 'I'm afraid we have no beer.'

Priestman smiled at the man, wishing that his pupils had such cultured English accents. 'A gin and tonic?'

'You see, I'm afraid we don't serve alcohol. Only soft drinks.'

'Could I send for some from an off-licence?'

'I'm afraid this is a holy day. They would be shut. In the bigger towns you would be able to get some.'

'Have an orange juice, and come and join us,' called the man at the table.

'I'm Harold,' the man said as Priestman joined them. 'And that's Mr Clive Clive.' He indicated a man with the build of a jockey and the screwed-up face of an alcoholic.

'You don't care 'bout the music,' said Mr Clive Clive. He blinked, and twitched his head.

'And that's Robert Lord,' said Harold indicating a fat man slumped in his chair, and beaming fixedly with wide red eyes. Above him hung a cartoon of a man and woman on the grass beside a waterfall. The caption read: 'Lovers' leap – Packmari'.

'Have a chota peg, burra sahib,' said Harold pouring something thick into Priestman's orange juice. It tasted oily. Priestman revolved his glass. 'Just out from Blighty?'

'Where? Oh, England. Yes. And where are you from?'

'The gentleman asks where you're from, Clive Squared?'

'I'm headin' for the las' round-up,' sang Mr Clive. 'You don't care for the music.' He raised his chin so that his lips met his nose.

'Stow it, Clive,' snapped Harold. 'Where are we from, Roberts?' The fat man continued to beam, but said nothing. 'Up the junction. That's where we're bloody from. Half-way between nowhere, that's what.'

'Oh give me a home where the buffalo roam, and. . .'

'I told you! Bloody stow it, Clive man,' said Harold.

'Well, thanks for the drink. Must be off,' said Priestman, smiling and getting up.

'What's the matter?' asked Harold. 'Anglo-Indians not good enough for you? What are you so proud of then? Your bloody Labour government of lechers and pooves? Nice mess you landed us in, Mr bloody Attlee! Clear out, then. Go off and shufti bint!'

'Didn' care for the music,' said the little man as Priestman left. 'Pale hands I love you, beside the Shalimar. Where are you now? Where are, are. . .'

'Shut that row, or I'll shut your face!'

Priestman stood on the hotel steps, gulping in the fresh, slightly misty air. A neat, moustached army lieutenant stood near him, one foot on his roll of bedding.

'Absolute hell-hole, what? Damn night train won't go for three hours.'

'Ah,' said Priestman.

'Thank God this place isn't like the real India. You've seen the big towns? No? Seen the new steel mills and the dams? No? You should. Progress. But not without discipline. Look at that scruffy crowd of tonga-wallahs and porters over there. No discipline. If anyone tells me one of those chaps is as good a man as I am, I'll knock him down. Care for a chukka of snooker?'

'No thanks,' said Priestman, and hurried off into the quickly gathering night. Noticing a museum, he thought he might go in and look round. But it was shut. A notice on the door had once read 'Closed All Monday', but 'Monday' had been crossed out and 'Tiwesday (sacred to God of War)' written after it.

That evening the fort was covered in a mist thicker than before. There was a stillness over all. The monkeys sat huddled on the battlements and the temple. The school boys, who had earlier enjoyed the cool weather and the strangeness of the mist, now complained. It was reported that a leopard had been seen near the Junior School. Priestman and the principal's driver had repaired the car as best they could, and Priestman, feeling let down by the failure of the expedition, now considered how he could get away in the car alone and spend as long as it would take to find the village. Having made that decision, he settled down to prepare the lesson for Amanti.

24

Amanti came unannounced through the door at about ten o'clock – earlier than he had expected.

'So you're not swimming tonight either?' laughed Priestman making breast-stroke movements with his arms.

'Not swimming, brrh,' shivered Amanti wrapping the blanket tighter round her. 'I am bad.' She frowned and screwed up her face and felt her body with distaste to indicate that she felt dirty.

'Never mind. I'll make us both some good, hot coffee. Bring me some water please.'

'Yes, sir.'

'Yes, Edward.'

'Yes, Edward, Sahib, Mr Priestman, sir.' They both laughed. He watched her through the bathroom door as she filled the kettle, then stood frowning at the bath. 'Little water for swim.'

'Ah, but I haven't shown you the shower.' He went in and turned on the taps. 'There you are, monsoon rain at Christmas time.' She was delighted with the water pattering into the bath, and held her hands under it rubbing them together. 'I know. You have a quick shower while I make coffee. Here's a towel, there's soap.' Amanti looked at him incredulously. 'Two minutes only. Then we will drink hot coffee and you will be happy and clean and you will learn well.' He went to his bed, and taking off a blanket hung it over the open doorway. 'Goodbye,' he added as he made the final adjustment to the blanket, and waving to her that he was going away, he went into the living room.

As he plugged in the kettle, he heard the sound of the running water change, then her gasping and stamping in the bath. While he was spooning the coffee powder into the cups, the verandah door burst open, and Priestman was confonted by Ram Swarup and six or eight servants carrying sticks.

Seeing Priestman calmly making coffee, they hesitated and jostled one another in embarrassment. But the one called Garap, who had been Macgregor's servant, stepped forward, and puffing out his chest and raising his stick, cried: 'Where girl Ram Swarup, bastard English?'

'Get out, all of you!' shouted Priestman, waving his arms and taking several steps towards them. They fell back a little. Ram Swarup came forward, and getting down on his knees, wailed, 'Amanti, sahib.'

Amanti came out of the bedroom running. She burst angrily through the group, pushing them roughly aside, and rushed outside. The men turned to confront Priestman.

'Sahib, sahib,' cried Ram Swarup, holding out his hands as though asking for an explanation.

'I teach her, Ram Swarup. Read.' Priestman held an imaginary book in front of him moving his head from side to side over it.

'Bastard!' yelled the man Garap and aimed a blow at Priestman. In grabbing the man's stick, Priestman stepped forward and accidentally stood on Garap's foot, so that he fell twisting his ankle and moaning in pain. The others fell back in silence.

And in the silence, they heard Amanti's cry of pain and bewilderment.

Priestman twirled the stick before him and burst through the group of gaping men. Following the sound of her moaning, he came to where Amanti lay on the path.

'Nag Rajah. Nag Rajah,' she sobbed, her eyes staring in amazement at Priestman.

'Snake, sahib, snake,' said little Choti Lal, Ram Swarup's helper, and grinned.

For a moment Priestman thought of carrying her to the nurse's clinic. Then he pushed aside the men who had gathered round, their mouths open, and ran back to his rooms. He found the spare keys to the principal's car, grabbed two bundles of bank-notes from a drawer, picked up the blanket from the floor by the bathroom door, and ran back.

The men still stood apparently paralysed around Amanti.

163

Cries of enquiry came from the servants' quarters, and the voice of a boy came from a nearby balcony shouting, 'What's up down there?' Priestman pushed the men aside, and picking up Amanti ran with her to the car. As he struggled with the keys, some of the men jostled him and clawed at his clothes. Pulling out a bundle of notes, Priestman began to throw them among the men. At first they did nothing, but as the man Garap hobbled round picking them all up, the others started to scramble for the money. Little Choti Lal, however, made a grab at the bundle in Priestman's hand. But Priestman pushed him onto his back.

Priestman got Amanti into the front passenger seat, and started the car. As it moved off, Ram Swarup, who had till then been standing looking vacant, ran forward and grabbed at the door handle. But he fell away as the car turned and gathered speed.

The mist was not too thick near the school buildings, but became dense between the Senior and Junior Schools. Amanti seemed to have fainted. She lolled up against him. After about two hundred yards he stopped the car, and examined her legs by the dim light of the dashboard. On her left heel was a dark swelling and a puncture from which blood oozed.

'Try to remember,' he said aloud. 'Should I cut it, suck it or leave it alone?' He put his mouth round the swelling, biting hard at it and trying to drag the poison out with his teeth, then spitting on to the floor. As he did so, he saw her naked thighs and belly. Frowning, he pulled the shift down to cover her. But the shift was soaking wet from her shower, and the blanket she wore was also damp. Taking a duster from the glove compartment, he tied it firmly below her left knee. Then he undressed her completely, wrapped the blanket he had brought round her, then put her blanket on last. As he put her feet back on to the car floor, her body convulsed and she made as if to vomit.

He sped off down the road, peering for the lights of the Junior School on his left. A man he assumed was the night watchman jumped out in front of the car, and waved his thick stick. Priestman accelerated and the man jumped back, his face looming unnaturally large through the windscreen.

Priestman missed the turning through the Monkey Gate, and only realized it when the ruined pile that had been the fort of

164

Sena Suj seemed to come forward to hit him. He reversed with difficulty among the large stones of the ruin. The mist was at its thickest during the descent from the Monkey Gate. Priestman had to put out one arm to prevent Amanti falling forward.

Once on level ground, he was in constant danger of colliding with tongas, cyclists and pedestrians. His hand was mostly on the horn. People shook their fists at him and cursed.

At the entrance to the town proper, Priestman stopped the car and asked the way to the hospital. A sympathetic group gathered round, but the directions he received were so confusing that eventually he threw up his hands and cried, 'I don't understand.' Then a youth who was more forward than the others, offered to conduct him, and climbed into the back seat. They made their way through the crowded bazaars, the youth leaning out of the window, slapping the sides of the car and shouting for people to get out of the way. Several times he asked Priestman to slow down so that he could talk to people he knew, and the interested people who gathered round made their progress more difficult.

'Come on, come on. Get out of the way!' shouted Priestman, adding to the boy, 'are you sure this is the right road?'

'Yes, yes. Drive on. Fast. Toot. Hooter, hooter!'

The road became more narrow, and then petered out at what seemed to be a long-deserted building site.

'Yes. Here. Very soon,' said the youth. 'I go one minute see my cousin-brother here.' He got out and ran off.

Amanti moaned and began to shiver violently.

'Oh God, God. This is all a mistake. Not this little girl. Not her. Just go back to what it was early today. Start again.' He reversed the car and started to go back up the road. The youth came back running and tried to open the front passenger door.

'Get off, you fool!' shouted Priestman and banged the half open door on to the youth's arm so that he let out a cry and fell back.

Turning left at the main road, Priestman asked the way after about fifty yards. He was told that the hospital was straight ahead about a mile further and on the right.

Priestman ran carrying Amanti up the hospital steps. Inside he was directed down a long corridor, and told to wait outside a door. He sat there, with Amanti propped beside him. After about a minute, when nobody appeared, he began to shout. A man popped his head out of the door, told him to be quiet and to come in. Priestman placed Amanti full length on several chairs, and put his coat under her head.

When he entered the office, the man had disappeared. There was a counter across the width of the office. At the back of the room a clerk was working on some papers at a desk. He looked up briefly at Priestman then back at his papers.

'Shop!' yelled Priestman banging the counter and groaning at the idiocy of the word.

The clerk looked up, nodded to Priestman and pointed at the door. The first man came out of the door with a bundle of papers which he took to the clerk. Then he came to the counter and gave Priestman a form printed badly in Hindi and English. Priestman started to fill it in, then thrust it aside saying, 'Look. Can't you see this is an emergency? I'll fill all that in later. Please get someone to see to the girl. I'll pay.' He pulled out a bundle of ten rupee notes and waved them at the man.

The man asked him to wait while he went and spoke to somebody behind the door. When nobody came after a further minute, Priestman left the room. Amanti had been sick on to the chairs and the floor. Two nurses came along the passage.

'I'll just get finished with the one in Ward Five, then I'll be with you,' said one of the nurses.

'I promise you, you will find it enchanting,' said the other.

As they were passing Priestman, he jumped up and spoke to them.

'Please help me. This girl has snake bite. She will die if she doesn't get help soon.'

'You have registered?' asked the nurse who had spoken first.

'Yes. Well, no. I don't know.'

'You must register in there,' said the second nurse, indicating the door.

'No. He should register at "Casualty Admissions",' said the first nurse.

'Excuse us,' said the other girl, and they walked off quickly down the passage. They met a man in a white coat who laughed and chatted with them. Priestman saw the nurses pointing him out. The doctor came up to him.

'What is this girl doing here? Why is there all this mess on the floor?'

'She's here because she has snake bite. The mess is there because she has been sick!'

'There is no need to shout. Nothing is gained by shouting. You are English?'

'Yes.'

'Where are you from?'

'London. Karatpore School.'

'You are a schoolmaster there. There is a clinic at the school. Has she been seen at the clinic?'

'No.'

'Why not? You should have a note of referral.'

'Look. There is no nurse at the clinic.'

'Why is that?' The doctor seemed very angry. The backs of his hands were hairy. Long hairs like thick fur lined the edges of his ears.

'I'm sorry to sound impatient. Could you possibly examine her please? I beg you to help.'

'She cannot be examined here.'

'You are a doctor, aren't you? I will pay.'

'Are you trying to bribe me?'

'Listen. I'll do whatever you say. Please do something now. Look she's having convulsions again.' Priestman ran to Amanti and tried to hold her still. He rearranged the blankets and replaced the coat. Her breathing was laboured. The doctor went nearer to her.

'She is having some convulsions,' he said. 'Breathing is affected. That is normal. Who applied that rag to her leg? It is useless. What type of snake was it?'

'I don't know. A cobra I think. Can't you give her some serum?'

'You must know what snake it was. Was it killed? The snake must always be killed. Those are the instructions specifically laid down by your people in London.'

'It was dark and misty. But I'm almost certain it was a cobra. Can't you tell what snake it was from the bite?'

The doctor looked more closely at Amanti's heel. 'Look at that!' he said angrily. 'There is contusion. Look at that. There is

damage to tissue. There is one puncture. Hold her up.'
Priestman did so. Amanti's head dropped sideways. 'There is
loss of muscular control. That is normal.'

'When you say "normal", do you mean that it's a good sign?'

'No, no. Why should you say that? It is normal in such cases.'

'Can't you give her an injection?'

'What injection?'

'Serum.'

'What serum? There is no serum. In Delhi or Bombay there
may be serum. But will it be effective? You do not know what
snake it is.' Amanti's breathing became more laboured. 'This
patient is in shock. She has not been reassured properly that she
may not die.'

'Why are you so bloody useless?'

'Why are you speaking like that to me?'

A man Priestman had not seen before came out of the office.
'Mr Priestman?' he asked.

Priestman lifted Amanti and ran with her down the corridor,
the two men in pursuit. The doctor caught up with him and tried
to stop him leaving. Priestman hit him hard on the side of the
head so that he fell down and cried out, 'Why did you do that?'

'Now the patient is in shock!' shouted Priestman. 'It is normal
in such cases.' The other man went to the assistance of the doctor
who was sitting with his back against the corridor wall, moaning.

Although the road to Bhonsa had no bordering kerb and no
trees to line it, it had the advantage of being straight and narrow.
The mist forced Priestman to keep to thirty miles per hour
maximum. Sometimes it seemed to Priestman that full
headlights were more effective, sometimes dipped, sometimes
no lights at all. For the first mile or so he juggled with the light
switches, then left the lights dipped for they showed up the
potholes. If he hit a pothole, Amanti's uneven breathing seemed
to stop, and she was liable to have a convulsion. He had re-tied
the tourniquet tighter. He drove with one arm around her,
whispering into her ear, 'It's alright, Amanti. Very good. Bring
me the book. You won't die. I will help you.' And sometimes he
tried to reassure her with the little Hindi he knew, '*Tikh hai.* . . .
Apka nag bahut achha hai – it's alright. Your snake is very
good.'

His main anxiety was that he would take the wrong turning at the place where the road forked. Then he remembered that since it was the right-hand fork which led to Bhonsa, he had only to drive on the right-hand side of the road to take the correct way. The fact of now driving on the legally wrong side of the road enhanced the nightmare quality of the journey.

'Now I have broken all the rules!' he shouted into the night. 'You swine,' he repeated at intervals. And each time he said those words, he was cursing some uncaring gods. 'You swine. And you do this to a child.' And he cursed himself as well, not for any folly he may have committed, but because it seemed to him that another Priestman or someone like him was following the car outside in the night, and was smiling down at them as though to say: 'Well, you wanted some action in your life. Now you have it. Something vital is really happening to you at last, here and now. You're playing a good part in the scene, aren't you? An instantly recognizable scene – the girl and the car and the night. Life has come to you at last. And you realize that life shows itself to you only through the nearness of death. And you are exhilarated, aren't you, as you dangerously increase speed, as you hold the girl closer to you than necessary? And is it possible that you are an angel of death?'

He had counted on the hill leading to Bhonsa to warn him of its proximity. But what had been steep to a cyclist in the sun, was not noticeable in a car at night. So he was in the village square of Bhonsa before he knew it. It was deserted. He drove round it and back along the road for another two hundred yards. Carrying Amanti, he stumbled through the mist towards the shelter of the blind holy man.

'Where are you, beggar? Where are you boy? If you want to sweat your lust out on your bride, go fetch your holy man. Come on, beggar, earn your rupees. Don't shiver so, child. Here, put on my coat, I'll help you. There; see how big it is, how funny you look!' He lay on top of her in the beggar's hollow, trying to keep her warm. 'And what could not you and I together, both outcastes in a land we love, have done? Beggar! You claimed three rupees. Here's a hundred – a thousand rupees for her life! Bring your stone, your vile brew. They say *Macbeth* is an unlucky play. Go to pretty child, would you play Cleopatra for me? I'll not watch it. No rosemary. No violets. But I forgot – *Hamlet* is not on the syllabus.'

Then, burying his face under Amanti's chin, he began to speak to her in clear Hindi with the voice of a small child: 'Why are those children crawling on their tummies, nanny? Those men were naughty to kick that poor man, weren't they? Is the little girl still sleeping on the road, nanny? Why did the dog pull at her leg? Edward was naughty to go outside, wasn't he? Now nanny will give Edward his bath.'

25

It was eight o'clock on a Monday morning in March. Already Mr Banglaratnam felt uncomfortably hot as he stood outside the doors of the school assembly hall, and shouted at the boys who were late.

'Hey, you boy. Run up, run up!' He bulged out his eyes, and jogged up and down to encourage them. 'Ah, Mr Panwar, Sen, I see. On your way to town to put to bed another splendid edition of the Review? Hindi section is expanding rapidly under your excellent editorship, Mr Sen. And your contribution about the King Lion of Bengal was so appreciated by the boys. Run up, you idle boy! What a pity you cannot come to assembly to hear Mr Agrawal address the boys on his work for the poor. Oh, this heat, already at eight o'clock!'

'I suppose,' said Panwar, 'that it would not be so hot this time of year in the south.'

'No, no. It would be very refreshing in the south. You must go to the south.'

'And in Throgton, Cheshire,' continued Panwar, 'it would be cool, I suppose?'

'Freezing. They are jumping up and down in their overcoats this minute.'

'Of course, it is there at this minute 2.30 a.m., which would make it even colder, I suppose.'

'Yes, yes. Run up you scoundrel!'

As Panwar and Arun Sen continued toward the Monkey Gate, Arun said: 'You are very bold. One day you will go too far with Banglaratnam. I no longer tease him. He is not entirely a fool.'

They were very hot by the time they had reached the town.

171

Before going to the printers, they decided to call in at the book-seller beside the bicycle shop, where they would be offered some tea.

In the shop they discussed the affair of Priestman.

'It always amazes me,' said Panwar, 'that the girl was alive when they found her.'

'Only in a small percentage of cases is enough venom passed to cause fatality,' said the book-seller. 'Mostly it is shock which kills. And she still will not speak?'

'Not a word,' said Arun Sen. 'If she does it will no doubt be in beautiful English. I would like to hear how he lay naked on her all night.'

'He was not naked,' said Panwar indignantly. 'The villagers told me that when they found him he was in his underclothes. He had simply taken the rest off to keep her warm.'

'My colleague,' said Arun Sen, 'still comes to the support of his ex-head of department even though the man is now a gibbering maniac. Always was, as far as I am concerned. But Panwar visited him in hospital in Delhi before they flew him back to England. He related the *Ramayana* by his bed. Such a friend.'

'He would have been your friend too, had you let him,' said Panwar sadly, and Arun frowned. 'The strangest thing was his obsession in the hospital with light. He kept talking about a light.'

'Lead kindly light,' sang Arun Sen.

'Perhaps the torches of the searching villagers?' suggested the book-seller.

'No,' continued Panwar. 'They were not found till morning, when two girls going to water their buffalo found them lying beside a pool. The villagers heard shouting in the night, but they thought it was evil spirits calling to each other. They say the country in that direction is an evil place. Strange lights have been seen. And another strange thing. When they found him, both his hands were clenched. They say he wept when they prised them open. In one hand they found perfectly round pebbles the size of pearls, and in the other just ordinary rough stones which had cut his palm.'

'I always maintained that nothing was to be expected of him save trouble,' said Arun Sen. 'And now what happens? On

172

Friday two large tins of battered English instant coffee arrive by sea for Panwar and me. And the customs duty cost us two weeks' salary at least.'

'So that is the last of him,' said the book-seller, and called out for the boy to hurry up with the tea.

'The last I heard,' said Panwar, 'was that his mother had written another letter to the principal. She said that Edward is now very calm, "radiant" she called it. But he doesn't recognize her. He speaks in riddles. One in particular she says makes him very happy. It goes, "those that come, go away again". Then he laughs. What do you think it could mean?'

'Anything you like it to mean,' said the shop-keeper getting up impatiently. 'But why all this fuss about one little reactionary Englishman?' The book-seller wiped his face, and turned on a fan.

'But he meant well. He was a good man,' said Panwar.

'So what does that matter?' said the book-seller. 'This man is good, that one is bad, the other is middling. Now your other good man, Agrawal, what will his goodness matter when they come for him? He is another sad case. His peaceful revolution is doomed. There is no time. It will all be swept away in a few years. They will bring him to trial as an enemy of the people, who will rush through the streets howling for his blood. He will confess and be shot quietly without fuss.'

'And what is your opinion of that?' asked Panwar.

'My opinion? I have no opinions. What is the use of opinions? It will happen, that is all. And as for your little episode of one reactionary rather stupid Englishman, it is a matter of no importance. History had simply passed him by.'

'Meanwhile,' said Panwar softly, and almost to himself, 'the children stop crawling forward through the dust, and begin to eat it.'

'Let us talk about something more interesting. Ah, the tea!'

After assembly, Agrawal sat in the principal's office in the school buildings. He had addressed the boys about the duty of the rich and well educated to help their less fortunate countrymen.

'Do you think anything of what I said sank in?' he asked the

173

principal. Agrawal seemed depressed and less confident.

'How could it not sink in? You are such an example to us all.'

'Of course,' replied Agrawal absently. Already at nine o'clock the little office was hot and stuffy, as though it had not recovered from the battering of the sun the day before. After the clamour of the boys rushing into their classrooms, a quiet had descended on the fort. The steady *tonk, tonk* of a coppersmith bird heralded the approach of the real heat. The monotonous sound wearied the two men, reminding them of the air shimmering above the rocks outside and of the brown grass flattened among them as though by the passing of many hammers. 'Sometimes,' continued Agrawal, 'I feel that India is a mistake – a sort of waste-bin, an unwanted appendix to that vast land mass from Europe to China.' He indicated a map of the world on the wall.

'Allah made hell, so why make India?' quoted the principal.

'Yes. The idea is not new. And I am getting old.' He looked above the principal's head to a touched-up portrait of Nehru gazing firmly to the East. 'Nobody wants us. We are kept out of charity. And I have not the calmness of Gandhiji.' He looked at another wall, smiling at the photograph of the little, bent figure striding along a road with one foot strangely upturned before it hit the surface. 'Such a long stride for such a small man. You know I have not done spinning for three weeks. I have broken my promise to him.'

'He would forgive,' said the principal.

'That is why I feel so sad. If I did nothing from now till the end of my days, he would forgive. Perhaps we cannot afford such forgiveness any longer.'

'Something has surely upset you. You are revered throughout the land. If you doubt yourself, what will happen to us?'

Agrawal tutted at the compliment. 'But I wish you had told me before this morning of this dreadful business with Edward. You should have sent for me.'

'It was all so sudden,' sighed the principal. 'We hardly knew what we were doing.' He looked distressed at the memory and wiped his forehead.

'To talk of it must be distressing to you. But you are right. Something has upset me. You know that Edward gave me the names of the village children he said he had met and talked with,

174

and you remember how he described the village. . . Well, I have found the village.'

'You mean it exists, not a few miles from here? This is terrible. What is to be done?'

'No, wait, please. On my latest trip to Orissa province, I visited our schools and ashrams. And you know there is usually a village attached to these centres. Well, at one of the villages I was walking down the main street, not thinking about it you understand, when I was suddenly struck by its similarity to the arrangement which Edward had described. I took out the list of names he had given me. I enquired of the villagers. Then I began to realize what had happened as the evidence built up. For example, one man said, "Yes, I have a daughter by that name who has a poor leg." Then another said, "And I have a son by that name who is blind in the left eye." And there were other similarities. For a while I could not understand, and then it came to me with horror that Edward had described to me not the village as it is now, but as it will be in ten or fifteen years' time. And if our thriving model village is like that, what will be the plight of the rest of India? And it was given to Edward to have that vision of the future and to pass it on to me!'

'Come now, Agrawal Sahib. This terrible business has really upset you. There must be hundreds of villages in that province where people have the same names and such common disabilities. How can you possibly say this village is the one?'

'Well, well, you may be right. An old man's idle fears. I am too idle these days and too much alone. Let us pray that you are right. Now I must go and visit my friend Ram Swarup and his daughter.'

They walked out of the little office into the blinding light, and saw a boy dodge behind a pillar.

'Here you boy!' said the principal. 'Is that you, Ashok?'

'Now,' thought Agrawal, 'if only this boy would come forward and say, "I did not go in to class, sir, because I wished to ask Mr Agrawal how I could help. I wished to tell him that I intend to study in the West, then return to help the poor." And I shall say, "Come to me when you return," and I shall put my hand upon his head, and I will feel his purpose flow into me and I shall not despair.' But the boy had vanished.

175

'That boy,' said the principal as they walked on, 'is one of the wild ones. He will never learn. But I understand he was fond of poor Edward. You know, the boys became very unruly after the affair of Edward. It unsettled them. One night, a whole crowd of them turned the cannon round so that it faced over the plain.'

'Ah, a symbolic gesture,' sighed Agrawal.

'But the next evening, they pushed it over the edge. You can see from here that it is gone.' The principal shielded his eyes and pointed.

'Now that is more like boys!' Agrawal smiled and nodded. 'And how is the girl? I suppose there is no question of marriage now?'

'No. That is all finished. I am told that she just sits alone. She will not speak, though they say she understands. She never smiles. She is ostracized by the others. They consider her unlucky, I suppose. But the most amazing thing is that she can now read English a little. Someone must be helping her. And all the time she will not be parted from a simple little geography book. I can have her brought to you. It is so tiring for you to walk in this heat.'

'No, I shall go to them.'

'You know they are quite well off. Edward's mother has been very generous. So I will see you at lunch.' The principal went back to his office.

Agrawal continued past the water tank, and turned down the path leading to the servants' quarters. He spoke to Ram Swarup, who accompanied him to the tree near the water tap where Amanti sat alone with her book. Agrawal sat with her for an hour. He then spoke again with Ram Swarup, and returned to the principal's bungalow.

At lunch, Agrawal was much more cheerful and the principal wondered what had effected the change.

'The trouble with the English,' said Agrawal, waving an arm as though Priestman were still sitting in a nearby armchair, 'is that they are ferociously idealistic and fiendishly bored. They haven't got a big enough garden to play in, and they are so sick of making and selling things after two hundred years of being best at it, that now they are bad at it. And if they could only stop being embarrassed by the godliness in them, what could they not do?'

176

'You will bring out their godliness if anyone can.'

'I intend to have a jolly good try,' said Agrawal laughing. 'I cannot allow whole generations of Englishmen to go around boring themselves to death. After all, I had a large hand in chucking them out. One has some responsibility to their children.' He grinned.

'As for us, we are having no more Englishmen. But you knew the school will have to run down. After September there will in all probability be no more intake. Government has cut our subsidy. The Rajah is very hard up. I think he will have to give up his aeroplane.'

'Oh dear, he will be so lost. I must speak to him and reassure him about the future. He is such a good man. And now I will tell you my marvellous news.' Agrawal finished his meal, and sat back beaming at the principal. 'The little girl Amanti is to come with me. You look so surprised. Did not Gandhiji have adopted daughters to help him in his old age?'

'There were ugly rumours.'

'Of course. India thrives, or rather does not thrive, on ugly rumours. Well, she and I will change all that. Together we will bring rumours of good news. She is a worry to her parents. They are delighted with the idea. She will be a treasure to me. How bright she is! How she perked up during our little chat! She will speak before long.'

Later, in the cool of the evening, the frail old man could be seen walking out of the school chatting happily to Amanti by his side. He stumbled slightly near the ruined Monkey Gate, and asked for her arm. She gave him her support, and smiling at each other, they continued on their way down to the railway station.